'You are insufferable!' Penny stormed.

'You don't think I'm any use for anything, do you?'

'You're good for this,' Josh murmured hoarsely. Then, crushing her hard up against him, he kissed her full on the mouth. For the space of five heartbeats Penny felt as if she were suspended outside time.

'I hate you,' she said weakly.

She felt rather than heard his throaty chuckle of amusement. 'Tell me that as if you mean it and maybe I'll believe you.'

Dear Reader

There's something different about Mills & Boon romances! From now on, in the front pages of all our stories, you'll find a short extract to tempt you to read on, a biography about the author and a letter from the editor, all of which we hope will welcome you to our heart-warming world of romance. What's more, if you've got any comments or suggestions to make about Mills & Boon's stories, drop us a line; we'll be glad to hear from you.

See you next month!

The Editor

Angela Devine grew up in Tasmania surrounded by forests, mountains and wild seas, so she dislikes big cities. Before taking up writing, she worked as a teacher, librarian and university lecturer. As a young mother and Ph.D. student, she read romantic fiction for fun and later decided it would be even more fun to write it. She is married with four children, loves chocolate and Twinings teas and hates ironing. Her current hobbies are gardening, bushwalking, travelling and classical music.

PLANTATION SUMMER

BY

ANGELA DEVINE

MILLS & BOON LIMITED
ETON HOUSE   18-24 PARADISE ROAD
RICHMOND   SURREY   TW9 1SR

*First published in Great Britain 1992
by Mills & Boon Limited*

© Angela Devine 1992

*Australian copyright 1992
Philippine copyright 1992
This edition 1992*

ISBN 0 263 77551 8

*Set in Times Roman 10 on 10½ pt.
93-9206-59611 C*

Made and printed in Great Britain

CHAPTER ONE

IT WAS like a jungle. On the banks above the river, green
trees and bushes grew in a dense mass and the air was
as steamy as in any Turkish bath. Penny stretched
drowsily and blinked. After the long flight from Australia
weariness was beginning to set in, and this secluded
backwater of the Black River seemed like a good place
to park the car and take a break. Winding down the
window, she pushed back her thick, corn-coloured hair
and gave a sigh of pure bliss as warm air rushed in. It
might be ninety-five degrees in the shade and humid into
the bargain, but she wasn't worried by it. Her slim,
tanned figure was clad in the minimum possible amount
of clothing. Loose peach-coloured shorts, a matching
striped white and peach halter-necked top and white
sandals allowed her to ignore the heat and concentrate
on the view. And it was certainly a view worth looking
at. Down below her lay one of the largest gladiolus farms
in South Carolina.

The banks beside the river were covered in a patchwork
quilt of vibrantly coloured flowers. Scarlet and gold and
white, the gladioli gleamed against their green setting in
the late afternoon sun. And above them a mist of fine
rainbows danced in the showers from the sprinklers.
Penny smiled wryly, imagining the comments her Art
School principal would make if he could see it. 'Too
much like a chocolate box to be real!' he would say
scathingly. 'Don't waste your time, girl!' But it *was* real
and well worth a closer look, even if she had to trespass
to reach it. Feeling slightly guilty, Penny climbed out of
the hire car, cast a quick look over her shoulder, then
squeezed through the fence at the edge of the road. In
for a penny, in for a pound, she thought. After all, this

entire American trip was completely out of character for
her. And if she was going to do crazy, impulsive things,
she might as well add trespassing to the list. Besides, a
brisk walk might wake her up a bit.

For the next ten minutes, she trailed rapturously
through the spearlike green plants, revelling in the gold
and orange and scarlet blooms. The fine mist from the
sprinklers fell in a cool drizzle on her hot skin, and a
mood of dreamy contentment settled on her. After the
cramped boredom of the long flight from Australia and
two hours of solid driving, it was sheer bliss to wander
through this picturesque field. But before long an even
more picturesque sight caught her eye.

'Oh, how pretty!' she breathed, as she reached the
edge of the planted area. 'I'd love to paint that.'

Down below, the river flowed away like green glass
between the overhanging trees. The path leading down
to the river was damp and slippery and tangled with
undergrowth, but Penny hesitated only for a moment.
Then, hitching her bag firmly over her shoulder, she
began to scramble downwards. She had only gone two
or three paces when she slipped and smeared her shorts
with mud. Gasping with laughter and dismay, she stag-
gered to her feet and continued on. But just as she
reached the water's edge, a harsh voice cut through the
air behind her.

'Hold it right there,' said the voice, soft with menace.
'Just turn around real slow and don't make any sudden
moves. I got a gun.'

Terror flowed through Penny's veins like iced water.
Her legs began to shake and her heart pounded so furiously that she thought it would leap right out of her
chest. Yet somehow, like a ballerina pirouetting in slow
motion, she managed to turn and face the intruder who
threatened her.

She had a confused impression of a tall, powerfully
built man of about thirty-five standing with his muscular legs apart and his tanned cheek resting against the

barrel of a rifle. Glossy dark hair fell over his forehead and he had one eye squeezed against the rifle sights. The other glared downwards, green and pitiless and unwinking. Penny let out a soft moan of fear, and at that moment two things happened. The gun discharged, and Penny flung herself sideways and hit the ground.

Her teeth jarred with the impact, but she was up in an instant and running like a startled deer towards the bank which led up to the road and safety. She didn't dare head for the path, where the man was still standing, but she flung herself at another part of the slope and began to scramble upwards, sobbing with terror.

'Stop!' roared the man.

Penny's only response was a frenzied babble. Glancing back, she saw the man set down his gun and run after her. With a stifled shriek she clawed at the green kudzu vines that carpeted the bank and tried to haul herself out of reach. Then suddenly she was on her feet again and bounding up the slope like a mountain goat. Hope soared in her breast, sending the adrenalin pumping through her entire body. She was going to make it! Then a piece of rotten wood gave way under her foot and a stabbing pain shot through her ankle. With a cry of dismay, she fell flat on her face amid the green vine. Writhing desperately, she managed to turn over, and saw her pursuer loping easily up the bank towards her.

'Don't shoot!' she begged, cowering into the bank with her hands over her eyes.

'Don't what?' he demanded in a tone that was halfway between annoyance and amusement.

'Shoot!' repeated Penny in a quavering voice.

There was no mistaking the amusement this time. Her tormentor gave a low growl of laughter.

'Do y'all really shoot trespassers where you come from?' he enquired in a tone of mild disbelief.

Penny lowered her hands and caught a glimpse of a suntanned face with a square jaw, white teeth gleaming in a sardonic smile and the clearest green eyes she had

ever seen. The expression in those eyes sent a tremor of
doubt through her. Mocking, arrogant, infuriatingly
direct, they did not seem to be the eyes of a maniac who
used young women for target practice.

'No, they don't,' she retorted defensively. 'But obviously you do here. You've tried to shoot me already.'

'Oh, no, ma'am,' replied her attacker coolly. 'I beg
your pardon, but I'm reckoned to be one of the best
shots in Williamsburg County and I couldn't have missed
you at that range. What I was shooting was this little
critter here.'

He strode swiftly back down the bank and, picking
up a long stick, whipped something into the air. Something long and limp with brown, scaly skin and an orange
underbelly. Penny took a quick glance and shuddered.

'W-what is it?' she faltered.

'A water moccasin,' he replied curtly. 'One of the
deadliest snakes we have in these parts. You were just
about to step on it when I arrived. You know, you're
pretty lucky I showed up when I did.'

He flung the dead snake into the undergrowth and
stood with his hands on his hips, eyeing her complacently. Something about his air of smug self-satisfaction
infuriated her. It was easy enough for him to stand there
handsome and self-assured in his open-necked white shirt
and immaculate green shorts, looking cool and masterful. He hadn't been frightened out of his wits and
hurt into the bargain.

'Yes, tremendously lucky,' she retorted sourly. 'Just
think, I might have never known the thrill of staring
down the barrel of a gun if you hadn't arrived when you
did.'

His mouth hardened.

'There are some women who might just say "thank
you" when a guy saved their lives,' he reminded her
provocatively.

'No doubt,' she snapped. 'There are some women who spend every minute of their lives kowtowing to men. I just don't happen to be one of them.'

'Is that right? Well, I was going to offer you a hand climbing up this bank, but if you're so all-fired independent, I guess you'd rather do it yourself. Now, if you'll excuse me, I'm leaving. I got work to do.'

'Fine with me,' replied Penny, her eyes glinting dangerously.

Anger flashed between them like summer lightning. But something else travelled with it. As she glared at the muscular dark-haired Southerner with the grim jaw and the narrowed eyes, Penny felt an unwilling stab of desire. Hot and treacherous and unwelcome, it flooded through her entire body. Damn the man! she thought irritably. Whoever he was, he didn't just look as if he owned the place. He looked as if he was master of the entire planet. Well, he needn't think Penny Owen was going to fall at his feet just because he was good-looking and confident. Gritting her teeth, she took a step forward. And fell whimpering at his feet.

'What is it?' he demanded in a voice sharp with concern.

Penny doubled up, gasping, as the pain subsided in her injured ankle.

'Nothing,' she groaned. 'I'm just swooning with gratitude, that's all!'

He swore softly and crouched in the tangled undergrowth beside her.

'This is no time for wisecracks!' he growled. 'Let me see that ankle.'

His brown hands were surprisingly gentle as he sat down and drew her injured foot across his thighs. Penny flushed self-consciously as she felt the rough, dark hair on his legs brush against her soft skin. Desperately she sat up and tried to draw her foot away.

'What is it?' he demanded.

'Nothing. I'm perfectly all right,' she said primly. 'If you'll just give me your arm, I'm sure I can get up the bank. And I have a hire car waiting by the roadside.'

'I don't give a good goddamn if you've got a Sherman tank waiting by the roadside,' he retorted. 'You're not going anywhere until I check that ankle.'

'But you can't!' wailed Penny. 'I don't even know you!'

A slow smile spread over the stranger's face. A smile that lent a surprising charm to his rather craggy features.

'Oh, I see,' he murmured in his soft Southern drawl. 'You're a properly brought up young lady and you don't allow men to handle you until you've been introduced. Is that it?'

Penny ground her teeth.

'Something like that,' she admitted in a choking voice. 'Now kindly let me go.'

His fingers touched her calf, softly, caressingly for a brief, fleeting moment.

'Oh, I believe I can do better than that,' he said teasingly. 'I guess I'll just introduce myself. My name is Josh Miller and these are my fields. I also have a plantation of three thousand and some odd acres about half a mile over yonder. I raise cotton and soybeans and I employ about a hundred people. What else? I was born and raised about fifty miles from here and educated at Clemson. I have a mama and a daddy, a brother and a sister. I belong to the local Moose Lodge, play golf at Myrtle Beach, and I make the best fried chicken south of the Mason-Dixon Line. Will that do, or should I call and get a reference from my old Sunday school teacher too?'

'That will do,' said Penny in a smouldering voice.

'Great,' smiled Josh Miller, rubbing his hands together. 'So now do I get to handle you?'

Although his touch was gentle, his first tentative rotation of her ankle brought tears to Penny's eyes. She caught her breath and bit her lip.

'So where do you come from?' he asked, trying to distract her from the pain. 'You can't be a Southerner, with an accent like that. I'll bet you're not even American.'

'No, I'm not,' panted Penny, fighting back the tears as he bent her foot slowly forward. 'I'm from Australia.'

'Australia! That's really far away! What's your name, honey?' asked Josh.

She took a swift uneven breath as his fingers probed her swollen flesh.

'Penny Owen,' she said.

'And what in the world are you doing in Williamsburg County?'

'I've inherited some property here,' she explained.

'Is that right? What kind of property?'

'Just a small house and a few acres of land. You see, my father was an American, but I never really knew him. He and my mother split up before I was even born, and I was always curious about him. Then about a month ago I had a letter from a lawyer in Charleston saying my father had died last year and left me this place. That really shook me. I'd always planned to come to the States one day and meet my father, and suddenly I found that time had run out. But it still seemed important to come and see the place where he used to live. Rather like making a pilgrimage, in a way. I was just trying to find it when I had to stop, but it must be quite close to here.'

Josh frowned thoughtfully. The movement set the fine lines around his eyes in motion and his face kindled as he looked around him.

'Well, Williamsburg County is a mighty fine place to own property,' he said in a voice vibrant with feeling. 'Some of the best people in the world live here and you can grow pretty well anything, the land's so fertile. So what are you going to do with this place you've inherited?'

Penny shook her head in a dazed fashion.

'I have no idea,' she admitted, spreading her hands. 'I only flew in from Australia this morning and I haven't even seen the place yet. But I was hoping to stay in the house tonight.'

Josh set her foot down and brushed his hands. Then he took a quick look at his watch.

'Well, there's not a hope of that now,' he remarked crisply. 'I'd say there's every chance you'll be spending the night in a hospital ward. That ankle looks to me as if it could be broken.'

'Broken?' wailed Penny in dismay. 'Oh, no! That will ruin everything!'

He shrugged.

'Well, if you hadn't run off like that, it wouldn't have happened,' he snapped in an exasperated voice. 'Biggest damn fool thing I ever saw!'

'Is that so?' she retorted hotly. 'Well, if you ask me, it's a pretty damn fool thing to go waving loaded guns at total strangers so that they think you're some kind of homicidal maniac!'

'Homicidal maniac!' echoed Josh wrathfully. 'Do I look like a homicidal maniac?'

'Yes!' snapped Penny.

His jaw tightened and his eyes flashed sparks.

'Look, I don't have time to stand around talking such foolishness,' he growled. 'I'm a busy man, Miss Penny, so let me just lift you up and take you to the hospital in Kingswood. Then I can get back to work.'

He crouched to scoop her up, but she struggled out of reach as energetically as if a whole nest of water moccasins were pursuing her.

'That won't be necessary!' she exclaimed through clenched teeth. 'I can manage perfectly well on my own, thank you!'

'Is that right?' drawled Josh. 'Well, I don't happen to agree with you, ma'am, so I think you'd better just give in. You were hurt on Miller land and I figure that it's my responsibility to take care of you. Now are you going to let me carry you nice and easy, or do I have to sling you over my shoulder like a sack of potatoes?'

She gave a low gasp of rage.

'You wouldn't dare!' she hissed.

A look of unholy amusement gleamed in Josh's green eyes.

'Well now, if there's one thing I can't resist, it's a challenge!' he said throatily.

And before Penny could move a muscle, his strong brown hands caught her under the armpits and hoisted her into the air. She gave a single outraged squeal of protest, then she found herself hanging upside down over his shoulder as he loped effortlessly up the bank.

'Put me down!' she shrieked, pummelling ineffectually on his muscular back. 'Put me down! Do you hear me?'

She might as well have pounded on a tree-trunk. Josh simply tightened his grip on her scantily clad rear and chuckled appreciatively. Only when they reached a gleaming BMW by the roadside did he come to a halt. Swinging open the car door, he deposited her carefully in the plush interior.

'Best-looking sack of potatoes I ever did carry,' he remarked gravely.

She was still swearing vengeance when he strode off down the hill to retrieve his rifle.

'OK, honey, next stop Kingswood Hospital,' he promised cheerfully as he came back and climbed into the driver's seat. Then he pressed a lever. 'Is this cool enough for you?'

Penny was grateful for the sudden current of chill breeze from the air-conditioner, but not for anything would she admit it. Her lips set in a hard line and her jaw jutted out angrily.

'I asked you a question, ma'am,' murmured Josh in a dangerous voice. 'I think it would be good manners for you to answer it.'

'Good manners!' choked Penny. 'You're a fine one to talk about good manners! Or do you consider it good manners to go chasing young women around the countryside, flinging them over your shoulder and carrying them off wherever you please?'

He looked thoughtful for a moment.

'Yes, ma'am,' he agreed pleasantly, 'I guess I do. Mind you, they don't usually struggle as much as you did.'

Penny made a noise like a pricked balloon.

'You're impossible!' she exclaimed furiously. 'You're nothing but a modern-day pirate in a BMW!'

Josh looked pleased. His mouth creased into a sensual smile and he cast her a teasing look.

'Why, thank you, ma'am!' he said modestly, as if she had paid him some kind of compliment. 'A pirate, eh? That's really something.'

Penny heaved an exasperated sigh and gave up. The more she abused Josh Miller, the more he seemed to enjoy it. Well, the only thing she could do was ignore him totally. That would soon show him how little she respected him! But, oddly enough, she found it impossible to ignore Josh Miller totally. Her midriff still felt the firm pressure of his shoulder, and she could not help recalling the way her breasts had brushed against the rippling muscles in his back.

She stole a quick glance sideways and saw his lean brown thighs flecked with dark hair, the lazy strength of his hands resting on the steering-wheel, his powerful chiselled profile. Somehow that face held her gaze disturbingly, and she caught her breath. He's arrogant, she told herself. Tough, hateful, overbearing. And, true enough, there was·a streak of arrogance in the set of Josh's chin, the firm, determined mouth, the unwavering look in his green eyes as he stared down the road. As if he only had to decide he wanted something in order to have it, thought Penny with a twinge of resentment. And yet something about him unleashed a hot prickling sensation of longing deep inside her. Josh's

right hand reached out to the dashboard and her gaze
skittered hastily away. But he did not seem aware of her
scrutiny. Picking up a car phone, he juggled it up to
where his left hand held the steering-wheel and punched
in a string of numbers.

'Hello. McKendrick? This is Josh. I got me a parcel
of trouble here to deal with tonight. Some fool girl hurt
herself on my land and I got to drive her to Kingswood
Hospital. So you'll have to postpone that Moose Lodge
meeting about the funds for the high school air-
conditioning system. And tomorrow morning, if I'm not
down at the cotton fields by dawn, you get everybody,
and I mean everybody, to lay off the rows ready for
planting in the Crooked Branch field. Got it? Good. I'll
see y'all in the morning.'

Penny's ears burned as Josh set down the phone.
Parcel of trouble... fool girl, she thought with a sense
of outrage. How dared he? Instinctively she drew away
from him as if she had been stung and her injured ankle
struck the side of the car. She gave an involuntary yelp
of pain.

'Is that ankle hurting you?' demanded Josh with more
exasperation than pity in his voice. 'Hell, if they're busy
at the hospital we'll probably spend another hour waiting
in the emergency room before anyone has a chance to
treat it. And that's before we even think about dinner
or finding you somewhere to stay tonight. I guess I'd
better stop at the next store and buy you some frozen
peas.'

'I'm not hungry,' said Penny haughtily.

He gave a throaty chuckle.

'I meant for your ankle, not your stomach,' he explained. 'I played football in college, and you can take
it from me, frozen peas make a mighty good ice pack
in an emergency.'

Within five minutes he pulled in at a tiny village con-
sisting only of a gas station, church, general store and
four or five white wooden houses. When he emerged

from the store, he carried a pack of frozen peas. Penny sat stiffly, half dreading and half longing for the moment when he would open the car door and lay them gently on her injured flesh. Instead he simply climbed in the driver's door and tossed the packet carelessly at her.

'There you go!' he said.

'Thanks, Sir Galahad!' retorted Penny.

But surprisingly the frozen peas did still the fierce throbbing in her ankle. By now jet-lag, injury and exhaustion were taking their toll and, without even realising it, Penny slipped abruptly into a deep and dreamless sleep. She woke with a start when the car came to a halt beside a large red brick building. Raising her head, she realised that she had been lying propped against Josh's brawny shoulder.

'Did you have a comfortable ride?' teased Josh.

Confusion swept through her.

'I beg your pardon,' she replied in a chilly voice. 'I had no idea I was lying all over you.'

'Happens to me all the time,' he replied jauntily. 'Seems like women just can't help themselves.'

Penny shot him a poisonous look, but clamped her lips firmly shut. She was not going to be drawn into another exchange of fire with Josh Miller.

'Not going to bite, huh?' remarked Josh in a disappointed voice. 'Oh, well, if the fun's over, I guess we'd better just get you into the emergency room. Stay where you are and I'll come round and carry you.'

It was only a short distance from Josh's car to the emergency room, but the air was so heavy and oppressive that it was like moving through water. Grey clouds were massing overhead and summer lightning flashed in jagged zigzags across the sky. Somewhere in the distance they heard the boom and crash of thunder.

'Looks like we're in for a storm,' remarked Josh, eyeing the gathering clouds keenly. 'That's good. We can really do with the rain.'

'It's terrible!' exclaimed Penny crossly. 'Everything's
gone wrong. I'll have to stay around in this hospital for
hours, and when I finally do get out, it'll be pouring.
Oh, I wish I'd never come here!'

Josh nudged the emergency room doors open with one
powerful shoulder and suddenly they were inside the
welcome coolness of the hospital. He set Penny down
in a comfortable chair in the waiting-room and smoothed
back a stray tendril of her hair. Then he looked directly
at her, taking stock of her brimming eyes, the grim set
of her chin and the way her hands gripped the arms of
the chair. And for the first time he spoke to her without
teasing or criticising.

'Now don't take on like that, honey,' he murmured
in his soft Southern drawl. 'You're going to be just fine.
It's only that you're tired and all hurt up and you think
you got to cope with everything on your own. Well, you
don't. You just leave it all to me. I'll go see the nurse
about getting you admitted and then I'll find us both a
drink. OK?'

He patted her cheek, and that small gesture of tenderness pushed her over the brink. Tears spilled down
her face and her pansy brown eyes blurred suddenly as
she looked at him.

'OK,' she choked.

'Good girl.'

Did she imagine or really feel that warm, reassuring
squeeze on her knee? Before she could decide, Josh's
features returned to their normal impatient scowl.

'Give me your purse and your passport,' he demanded.

'What for?' asked Penny in alarm, clutching at her
bag and looking at him through a mist of tears.

He sighed.

'Because I'm an eccentric bag-snatcher who only likes
to rob his victims in broad daylight in front of witnesses,' he replied sarcastically. 'But just this once I'll
only use your belongings to arrange your hospital
admission.'

'Oh,' murmured Penny in a flustered voice. 'All right, then.'

She felt oddly disquieted as Josh lounged across to the desk with her bag. It was unnerving to have a total stranger taking charge of her life in such a high-handed fashion, even though it was a relief not to have to deal with all the red tape herself. Cringing inwardly, she heard him inform the nurse that she was twenty-four years old, a commercial artist, had full medical insurance and was suffering from a suspected fracture of the right ankle. There was nothing particularly private about any of these details, but Penny could not help resenting the confident way that Josh reeled them off. His air of being totally in control of the situation infuriated her, and she felt even more infuriated when she noticed the charm that he lavished on the receptionist. Gone were the exasperated voice and the unsmiling expression which had characterised his dealings with Penny, and in their place was a warm, sympathetic friendliness that soon had the busy nurse chatting animatedly to him. Hypocrite! thought Penny sourly. I'll bet he's only nice when he wants something. Sure enough, Josh soon glanced at his watch and asked the woman casually how long they would have to wait. I suppose he thinks she'll let us jump the queue, seethed Penny. But if that was Josh's hope, it was doomed to failure.

'I'm sorry, Mr Miller,' said the receptionist in a harried voice. 'We're really busy here tonight. There's bin a car wreck over by Grantlyville crossroads with four teenage boys in it. One of the doctors will do a preliminary examination on this young lady right away, but I imagine it'll be nearly an hour before they can see her in X-Ray.'

'Is there somewhere we can get coffee around here?' asked Josh.

'Yes, sir. There's a machine down the corridor yonder, but only get it for yourself, mind. Nothing for the patient, in case she needs surgery on that ankle.'

Josh nodded, then paused as a sudden thought struck him.

'Can I bring you some coffee too, ma'am?' he offered. 'If you're so busy, I'll bet you haven't had anything since lunchtime, have you?'

'Well, no, sir,' agreed the nurse. 'I ain't had anything, but don't you worry none about me—I'll be off duty before long. Still, it's real nice of you to bother.'

Penny glared resentfully at Josh as the woman gave him a conspiratorial smile. I wish she could see how nicely and charmingly he behaves towards me, she thought angrily. But then he's not trying to sweet-talk anything out of me, is he? I'm just a nuisance to him, so he's not likely to bother being polite to me. Sure enough, when Josh came striding back towards her, his voice was curt and held a hint of exasperation.

'You'll have to excuse me for a few minutes,' he said brusquely. 'I need a cup of coffee and I have one or two phone calls to make.'

'Yes, of course,' agreed Penny, dashing away the last of her tears with the back of her hand.

She was already feeling ashamed of her earlier outburst, and now she vowed to keep her troubled emotions under control. There was no point letting her annoyance about her injury and her hostility towards Josh overwhelm her. Infuriating as he was, he had at least had the decency to bring her to a good hospital. And it was probably only pain and shock that was making her feel such a turbulent readiness to burst into tears. All the same, it was a relief when an orderly took her away in a wheelchair to a curtained cubicle where a ginger-haired doctor soon appeared to examine her. The next ten minutes were excruciatingly painful and Penny had to summon all her willpower to avoid crying like a child. At last she was wheeled back to the waiting-room, but to her unreasoning dismay, Josh Miller still had not returned. He's probably got tired of waiting and left, thought Penny grimly. I suppose I ought to be pleased, but I'm just so tired, and everything's gone wrong. And at least Josh seemed to know what to do. He might even be quite a nice man really. Fighting down her disappointment, she smiled brightly at a middle-aged woman who had just taken a seat on a bench opposite her. The woman gave her a tremulous smile back and then choked on a sob.

'What is it?' asked Penny in dismay. 'Are you in pain? Shall I call a nurse?'

'Oh, no, honey, it's not that,' replied the woman, rolling a handkerchief into a ball between her hands. 'I'm just fine, but I'm worried about my boy Steve. He was the driver of that car that got wrecked over at Grantlyville, and I'm so afraid that he's bin hurt real bad. They won't let me see him yet and I don't know what to think. My name's Wilma Cox, by the way. But how about you, honey? What you in here for?'

Partly to distract the other woman, Penny introduced herself, and gave a heavily censored description of her encounter with both the water moccasin and Josh Miller.

'Oh, lordy, lordy!' exclaimed Mrs Cox. 'Well, if I were twenty years younger and forty pounds lighter, honey, I'd think it was just about worth spraining my ankle so I could be carried off by Josh Miller. Why, I declare, every young woman in the County is after that man! Although it looks like Brenda Sue Hartley has finally got him pinned down. Why, she had him leg-roped before he even knew what was happening, and I believe they're fixing to marry real soon. Well, she's a mighty handsome girl—rich, purty and sharp as a tack, even if she is a mite conceited. And the Hartleys are a real old family in these parts, just like the Millers. Her daddy's real big in the insurance business and they've got more money than they know what to do with. Yes, ma'am, I reckon that'll be the wedding of the season!'

Penny was shocked by the pang that went through her at this innocent revelation. So Josh Miller had a girl-friend, did he? Well, it was hardly surprising and certainly none of her business, but something about the news made her feel stunned. She thought of the way Josh had thrown her so casually over his shoulder, of the throbbing tide of longing that had swept through her at his touch, and she almost groaned aloud. No doubt he had found it very amusing to flirt lightheartedly with Penny Owen while Brenda Sue was waiting at home, rich, purty and sharp as a tack. Quite a nice man indeed! she thought savagely. How could she have been such a fool?

The door opened and Josh strode in, carrying a fragrant cup of coffee and a women's magazine, which he handed to Penny. She took it gingerly and gave him a look that smouldered with resentment.

'Thank you,' she said curtly.

His eyebrows shot up. Ignoring Penny, he turned to Mrs Cox.

'I'm real sorry to see you here, Mrs Cox,' he murmured. 'I heard about young Steve and I just hope it's nothing serious. Would you care for this coffee, ma'am? I can easily get myself some more.'

'Why, thank you, Mr Miller, you're a real gentleman,' said Mrs Cox gratefully. 'I don't believe there's a nicer man in the entire County.'

'You hear that, Penny?' demanded Josh smugly. 'Are you sure you don't want to join my fan club too?'

Penny cast him a glowering look. There he goes again! she thought furiously. Charming the life out of every female between the ages of eight and eighty. Except me.

'Quite sure,' she retorted acidly. 'I prefer civilised men. Like Conan the Barbarian.'

Mrs Cox looked puzzled and dismayed by this exchange of hostilities, but she was not left to wonder about it for long. Shortly afterwards, a doctor came and called her out of the waiting-room. She returned five minutes later, looking radiant.

'How did Steve go?' quizzed Josh. 'Nothing serious?'

'One broken leg and a fractured wrist,' replied Mrs Cox joyfully, 'but they'll be better in time for him to go back to college in the fall. And maybe now he's got to stay home, he'll actually study some!'

Penny smiled.

'That's wonderful!' she said sincerely, stretching out her hand to the older woman. 'I'm so pleased for you.'

Mrs Cox shook her hand vigorously.

'Well, y'all come over for dinner one night before you leave,' she invited. 'I'll give you my number and you just call me up once you're settled.'

'Thank you,' smiled Penny, accepting the hastily scribbled note which the older woman thrust at her.

'Miss Owen,' called a nurse. 'They're ready for you now in X-Ray.'

An hour dragged by as a radiologist took X-rays and developed them before sending them back to the doctor who had seen Penny in the emergency room. At last the short, ginger-haired intern poked his head around the curtain of the cubicle where Penny was waiting with Josh.

'Good news, Miss Owen,' he said cheerfully. 'There are no bones broken, but that's a mighty severe sprain you got there. I'll give you a shot of painkiller, but it'll make you pretty dopey once it takes effect. Do you have somebody to take care of you when you get out of here?'

Penny's lip quivered. In spite of the promise of pethidine, her ankle still throbbed violently. The exhaustion from her long journey suddenly swept over her in a wave, and for a moment she wanted to lay her head on someone's shoulder and howl.

'No,' she admitted forlornly.

With a few brisk movements the intern drew up the injection, swabbed her flesh and plunged the syringe in. Then he cast a swift, speculative look at Josh, who stood with his arms folded, drumming his fingers impatiently. The intern sighed.

'Well, I guess I could admit you to the hospital overnight for pain management,' he suggested sympathetically, staring down at his clipboard. 'You're not going to be able to manage alone, and that's a fact. I'll just check and see if there's a bed available.'

'Wait!'

The word cut through the air like a knife. Josh had stopped drumming his fingers and was standing with his hands on his hips, staring at Penny with the sort of resentful pity he might have shown to an abandoned puppy.

'Miss Owen can come home with me,' he said wearily.

'There's no need——' began Penny.

But it seemed as if nobody wanted to hear her opinion. The doctor was looking relieved, Josh was giving directions to an orderly with a set of crutches and somebody was holding open the doors to the car park. It seemed easier to give in than to argue.

'Thank you,' murmured Penny unhappily.

As the gleaming BMW slid silently out of the hospital car park, she laid her head against the window and groaned. For years she had dreamed of coming to America and finding her roots, but now the dream seemed to be turning into a nightmare. What she had always pictured was a loving reunion with her father, perhaps even a crowd of welcoming relatives. But the truth was that her father was dead. And in his place there was only this hostile stranger, who couldn't wait to be rid of her.

Sheet lighting flickered across the evening sky like a giant strobascope. In its sinister brightness Penny saw Josh hunched angrily forward over the steering-wheel, and a pang of regret shot through her. I shouldn't have come, she thought miserably. It was madness. But I won't stay. Just one quick look at Merivale to see where my father lived and then I'll put the place up for sale and go back to Sydney.

There was a sudden loud rumble of thunder. Then, with a violent crack, the sky split open. Rain poured on to the windscreen with all the force of a fire hose, and Josh clutched tightly at the wheel and peered intently at the road ahead.

'You OK?' he demanded above the roar of the storm.
'I can pull over, if you want. But I think if we just keep
going, I can get us out of trouble. Do you want to trust
me and let me do it my way?'

'Sure,' agreed Penny unhesitatingly.

And, as she said it, she realised it was true. Josh Miller
might be arrogant and domineering and entirely too
sensual for any woman's peace of mind, but she would
trust him with her life. It was as simple as that. With
that realisation, all Penny's tension drained away and a
sudden yawn overtook her.

'Do whatever you want,' she murmured drowsily, and
promptly fell asleep.

She was dimly conscious of the roaring and buffeting
of the storm and then of a long time when the only
sounds were the purr of the air-conditioning and the occasional swish of a passing car. But at last Josh shook
her by the shoulder.

'Wake up. We're home,' he told her.

There was pride in his voice—as well there might be,
thought Penny. Blinking as she surfaced from sleep, she
gazed out of the car window and wondered if she were
still dreaming. The rain had stopped and ahead of them
in the soft radiance of the rising moon was an avenue
of immense live oak trees, swathed in long scarves of
Spanish moss. At the end of the avenue was the most
beautiful house Penny had ever seen. It stood proudly
with four strong white columns supporting the front
porch, an iron lace balcony above the fanlight of the
entrance hall and two symmetrical wings of red brick on
either side. Whistling softly, Josh drove up the smooth
driveway and parked the car on a brick patio near the
back door.

'Well, here we are,' he said simply. 'I figured it would
be easier to get you in this way than to go up the front
steps. Just wait and I'll help you out.'

As he opened the car door a flood of night-time sensations assaulted Penny—the gurgling of rainwater in the

guttering, the smell of moist earth and sodden flowers, the cry of some night bird. Without hesitation Josh swept her into his arms and carried her to the kitchen door. She had a confused impression of comfortable rocking chairs and lush potted plants on the back porch, then Josh's key turned in the lock. Once inside, he set her down, steadying her with one arm, and felt for the light switch.

'Oh, shoot!' he exclaimed in annoyance. 'That darned storm must have blown a cable down. Stay right here and I'll get us some light.'

Penny felt her way cautiously into a rocking chair and sat down to wait. Before long a soft yellow glow lit the adjoining room.

'Well, I guess you'll be wanting some supper,' said Josh briskly. 'Come on in.'

Without even consulting her, he lifted her effortlessly and strode into the next room. Penny uttered a loud gasp. It was like stepping back in time. Josh had lit a kerosene lamp, and its glowing yellow light winked back from every surface. The huge gilt mirror that dominated one wall, the cascading chandelier that hung from the high ceiling, the lustrous silver and crystal on the dining table all shone with a soft reflected radiance. Setting Penny casually down in a high-backed mahogany dining chair, Josh lifted the lid from an ornate silver chafing dish and sniffed appreciatively. She caught the aroma of roast turkey with corn bread dressing, and her mouth watered.

'Well, let's eat,' urged Josh.

'There's only one place set,' protested Penny. 'I can't take your supper.'

He shrugged.

'Sarah McKendrick would be mighty insulted if I couldn't feed an entire army on any meal she set out for me,' he replied. 'And there are plenty of plates.'

Penny blinked as he thrust a table mat, Royal Doulton plate and a dazzling assortment of silver and crystal in front of her.

'Sarah McKendrick?' she repeated in a puzzled voice.

'My housekeeper. Her husband is my plantation manager and they have a cottage in back of the house here. Sarah's a mite persnickety, but I believe you'll enjoy her cooking.'

Penny did enjoy Sarah's cooking. The roast turkey was accompanied by rice and gravy, cranberry sauce, boiled okra, onions and corn, with a delicious pecan pie and whipped cream to follow. Penny savoured every morsel, but by the time Josh went into the kitchen to brew fresh coffee, her head was beginning to nod again. Josh returned with the coffee-pot to find her with her eyes closed and her cheek resting peacefully on her folded arms. His harsh features softened into an unwilling smile and he set down the coffee-pot on a silver trivet.

'Miss Penny, I don't believe you want coffee tonight,' he said, touching her shoulder. 'I believe you want a real good sleep.'

Penny's eyes opened drowsily.

'I'm sorry,' she murmured, 'it's forty hours since I flew out of Sydney and I just can't stay awake.'

Josh was no longer the maniac who had threatened her with a gun or the pirate who had flung her over his shoulder or the bully who had hustled her in and out of the hospital. He was simply a surprisingly warm smile in the lamplight, a strong pair of arms lifting her out of the chair and carrying her up a curving staircase into the shadows above. A man so powerful and protective that Penny's head lolled against his shoulder and she slept trustingly in his arms as they moved through the silent house. Until Josh's foot caught in the rag rug in the best guest-room.

'Damn!' he muttered, stumbling against the huge fourposter.

'Josh?' mumbled Penny.

Pain shot through her ankle and she woke with a start to find herself in a lamplit bedroom with flickering shadows on the walls.

'I didn't hurt you, did I?' demanded Josh.

'No,' she lied.

The fiery daggers of pain in her foot were easing, but she slowly realised that she was lying on a bed. A big bed. With Josh Miller half sprawled across her.

'Josh?' she whispered again.

Excitement coursed through her, swift, instinctive and unbidden. Raising her hand, she drew her finger down his face, feeling the roughness of evening stubble. Josh's eyes were dark and glittering in the lamplight as he stared down at her. Then his breath caught in his throat and he drew her hand to his lips and kissed it.

An exquisite, erotic torment flared through every nerve in Penny's body as she felt his warm, urgent lips on her skin. She tensed up, shuddering beneath their touch, and suddenly madness seemed to seize them both. Josh's next kiss was neither so brief nor so gentle. Hoisting himself on to the bed so that he lay full length beside her, he threaded his fingers through her hair and gathered her quivering body hard against him. Then he kissed her with a brutal, ravenous passion that made her ache with longing. Closing her eyes, she gave herself up to the warm, thrilling pressure of his mouth against hers, the sensual torment of his hands, the insistent virile warmth of his male body as he pressed her hard against him. For fully two minutes they lay like that, both throbbing with the need for a closer union.

Penny's breasts seemed to swell and tighten against the skimpy fabric of her halter-neck top, and she heard Josh's low groan of desire as his body strained against her. Then his fingers moved impatiently to the knot that confined her lush curves and suddenly she found her willpower. Her eyes fluttered open, dark with desire and the struggle to behave sensibly.

'No,' she whispered, fighting him off. 'No, Josh. We mustn't!'

CHAPTER TWO

PENNY woke slowly the following morning. At first she
was content to float in a dreamlike state, only half aware
of the immense four-poster bed with its lacy canopy, the
distant whirr of the air-conditioning, the crisp percale
sheets that smelled of rose petals. Home, she thought
blissfully, inhaling the fragrance and letting her gaze
wander over the heavy, dark furniture. She had always
imagined her father's house like this—a gracious
Southern mansion rich in history and with an atmos-
phere of quiet elegance.

Sighing, she turned over and prepared to snuggle
deeper into the broderie anglaise pillows. But the
movement sent a stab of agony through her injured ankle
and, with the returning pain, came returning con-
sciousness. Penny sat up in a sudden panic. This wasn't
her father's house! This place belonged to Josh Miller.
The man who had kissed her so violently last night...the
man who had tried to undress her.

With a sudden shock of resentment she looked down
and saw that she was wearing a white lacy nightdress
with a ribboned bodice. A low groan escaped her.
Evidently Josh had succeeded only too well, and, now
that she thought about it, vague memories came back
to her of that undignified tussle the night before. She
knew that Josh had kissed her and it was obvious that
he had undressed her too, but she was pretty certain that
nothing more had happened. Or had it? Dazed by
exhaustion from her long journey and the injection at
the hospital, she couldn't even be sure of that. Rage and
humiliation flooded through her entire body. How could
Josh Miller have taken advantage of her in such a ruthless
way?

28

At that moment the door burst open, and Penny sat
bolt upright with a murderous scowl. The man didn't
even have the decency to knock! But it wasn't Josh Miller
who stood framed in the doorway. It was a plump, grey-
haired woman in a floral pinafore with a vacuum cleaner
in one hand and a duster in the other. She paused on
the threshold with a ludicrous expression of dismay on
her face.

'Oh, lordy, lordy!' she cried. 'I'm sorry, ma'am, I had
no idea you were in here. Mr Josh didn't tell me. I'm
Sarah McKendrick, the housekeeper. I guess you're one
of Mr Josh's girlfriends from out of town, are you?'

'No, I am not!' retorted Penny indignantly. 'My name
is Penny Owen and I sprained my ankle on Mr Miller's
land yesterday. I had nowhere to go, so he invited me
back here for the night.'

Sarah's features creased into an exasperated smile.

'Well, ain't that just like Mr Josh?' she demanded.
'He's real generous and hospitable, but I tell you, ma'am,
he never explains nothing to nobody! That man is a law
unto himself, and if you're involved with him, you better
just scramble along and figure things out the best way
you can. Because he'll never tell you anything. Never
apologise, never explain, that's Mr Josh's way!'

It certainly is, thought Penny bitterly. If only he'd told
me there was a snake near my feet yesterday I'd never
have run away like that and sprained my ankle. And I
wouldn't be in this mess now. She sighed.

'Could you pass me my crutches, please?' she asked
in a subdued voice. 'I need to go to the bathroom.'

'Why, sure, honey!' cried Sarah, setting down her
vacuum cleaner and her duster. 'And after that I'll fix
you some breakfast. Mr Josh went out into the fields at
dawn and he won't be back until about two o'clock, so
you can have a real good rest this morning. And I don't
want you to worry about a thing.'

Penny did have a good rest, but even Sarah
McKendrick could not stop her worrying. And most of

her worries centred on Josh Miller. The real problem,
she told herself resentfully, is that I can't stand the man,
but I'm still drawn to him. If only I hadn't been crazy
enough to kiss him like that last night! But perhaps he'll
have the decency to pretend it never happened...

Unfortunately, when Sarah McKendrick helped her
into the dining-room shortly after two o'clock, it was
clear that decency was the last thing on Josh's mind. As
the housekeeper prudently withdrew, Josh let his gaze
slide admiringly down Penny's body. She was wearing
a white top which clung enticingly to her bosom and a
swirling floral skirt which showed off her shapely brown
legs. Both garments had been lent to her by Sarah, but
judging by their proportions, belonged to somebody a
good deal slimmer than the housekeeper.

'You look very nice,' murmured Josh approvingly.
Then the lines around his eyes crinkled with mischief.
'A whole lot better than you did in those muddy shorts
yesterday. Although not nearly so good as you looked
in nothing at all.'

Penny's cheeks burned.

'It was kind of Mrs McKendrick to lend these clothes
to me,' she said frigidly. 'I suppose they belong to one
of your "girlfriends from out of town". Or don't you
even remember?'

He grinned lazily.

'Well, no, I don't,' he admitted. 'Can't say as I really
notice their clothes much—only what's in them. But if
it makes you feel any happier, I've sent one of my men
to pick up your rented car and get your luggage, so you'll
soon have your own clothes back. Now what can I get
you to drink?'

He pulled out one of the heavy mahogany dining
chairs, helped Penny to ease herself on to its blue
needlepoint seat and took her crutches. Then he poured
a tall, dark-coloured drink from a frosted jug clinking
with ice cubes.

'You do drink iced tea, don't you?' he asked, settling himself casually into the chair at the head of the table with his long, muscular legs stretched out in front of him. 'I can ring Sarah if you'd prefer something else.'

'Iced tea will be fine,' agreed Penny hastily, dreading the need for any more encounters or explanations. All she wanted now was to get away from this place as fast as possible. 'Mr Miller, about moving to my own property——'

'The name's Josh,' he cut in firmly. 'And I don't aim to talk about that until we've eaten. Now what will you have? There's fried chicken, potato salad, coleslaw, green salad, pickled peaches, chocolate brownies...'

Only when they had both demolished large plates of food did Josh break the silence again.

'So tell me more about yourself,' he commanded, helping himself to more iced tea. 'What exactly do you do for a living?'

Penny wrinkled her nose.

'I draw soup cans mostly,' she admitted. 'And set up TV advertisements where lemons explode out of women's washing machines—all that sort of thing. I've been a commercial artist with an advertising agency for the last three years, ever since I finished art school.'

'But it's not what you really want to do?' urged Josh perceptively.

She shrugged.

'Not exactly,' she agreed. 'I'd really like to paint landscapes, but it's awfully hard to make a living doing that. And it's not as though I absolutely hate advertising work. I just wanted a change.'

'And that's why you came to the States?' demanded Josh.

Penny eyed him warily. Her motives for hopping on a plane to South Carolina were complex and private. Exploring the American side of her heritage was deeply important to her, but it was only half the story. And the other half was too raw, too painful, too humiliating to entrust to a total stranger. Especially a hostile stranger like Josh Miller. Her fingers tightened convulsively round the delicate crystal tea glass as she remembered the way her engagement to Simon Montgomery had broken up. Her mother's shocked reproaches, Mrs Montgomery's crude insults and Simon's outraged stupefaction all came sweeping back with brutal force.

Everybody had thought Penny Owen, who was nobody in particular, was doing very well for herself by marrying a company director of Gleeson's Advertising Agency. And they had all been totally thunderstruck when she called off the engagement only eight weeks before the wedding. Particularly since her only excuse was her slow realisation that she simply did not love Simon. A defiant spark of resentment flared up in her as she remembered her mother's tirades about security, trustworthy husbands and love not being the grand, spectacular marvel it was cracked up to be. Even worse had been Simon's hurt indignation and his mother's hysterical outburst in which she claimed that she had seen it coming all along. What could one expect but shabby behaviour when a girl came from a broken home and didn't even have a father willing to acknowledge her? Penny's mouth tightened at the thought of those spiteful insinuations of everything from bastardy to mental instability that Sonia Montgomery had flung at her. All right, perhaps she had behaved badly in waiting so long to tell Simon of her misgivings about loving him. Yet in spite of all the anguish it had caused, she had felt only relief at her refusal to go through with the marriage. Bride's nerves, they had called it charitably at first. And then self-indulgent foolishness. And finally sheer, bloody-minded obstinacy.

But while her own mother reasoned and cajoled and Simon's mother shrieked and reproached, Penny had remained shaken but immovable. She felt as if she had had a narrow escape, like some heedless young fish swimming into the wide open mouth of a net, only to

find it channelling her towards disaster. Of course there
had been a price to pay for regaining her freedom—pre-
sents to send back, embarrassing letters of explanation
to write, ruffled feathers to soothe. Fortunately her
mother had taken herself off almost immediately on a
long-postponed overseas holiday. Sonia Montgomery
had thrown herself into a whirl of cocktail parties and
society lunches at which she had blackened Penny's
character to anyone who would listen. And Simon, after
stiffly assuring Penny that her job at Gleeson's naturally
remained open to her for as long as she wanted it, had
soon consoled himself with a bright young female
executive in the Accounts Department. Oddly enough it
was Penny, the instigator of all the uproar, who had suf-
fered worst. Miserably convinced that she probably was
the irresponsible, flighty, unfeeling troublemaker that
they all seemed to consider her, she had moped around
her home, wondering if life would ever be bearable again.
The news of her legacy could not have come at a more
opportune time, and in spite of her sadness over her
father's death, she had felt a tremendous relief at
climbing aboard a plane and leaving the whole disastrous mess behind her. Yet she did not want to explain
any of this to Josh, so she simply gave him a small, taut
smile.

'Well, I came mainly for a change,' she said coolly.
'But also I had to do something about this property I've
inherited. I suppose I'll have to put it up for sale before
I go back to Sydney.'

Josh stroked his chin thoughtfully.

'You told me yesterday that you grew up in Australia,
but your daddy was American. Is that right?' he asked.

'Yes,' agreed Penny bleakly.

Her face shadowed, as it always did when she thought
about the father she had never known. Josh looked at
her keenly.

'Well, go on,' he urged.

'What do you mean?' she countered.

'How did your father come to be here in the States when you were growing up Down Under?'

Penny swallowed. Why should she tell him anything? she thought defiantly. Especially when he had been so rude and mocking earlier on. But he was looking at her with intent green eyes and his expression was no longer rude or mocking, simply thoughtful and encouraging. And she had the uncomfortable premonition that if she didn't reply, he would simply pass on to interrogating her coolly about her love life. So she chose the lesser of two evils.

'My parents split up before I was even born,' she explained unwillingly, 'and for years I knew nothing at all about my father. One of my mother's friends once let slip the fact that he came from South Carolina, but my mother always refused to discuss him. If I ever raised the issue, she would simply go very quiet and then change the subject. I think she felt that marrying him was the one big mistake she ever made in her life.'

Josh looked at her from under heavy dark brows.

'You're sure they were married, then?' he prompted quietly.

'Yes!' flashed Penny angrily. Her chin came up and her brown eyes blazed. 'Are you calling me a bastard?'

'No,' replied Josh peaceably. 'And it wouldn't matter to me if you were. I just thought it was one possible explanation of why your mama was so tight-lipped on the subject.'

'Well, it's the wrong one!' snapped Penny. 'I happen to know for a fact that they were married.'

'How?' asked Josh.

'When I was about twelve, I was going through a pile of old books in the basement for a church jumble sale. And instead of sorting them out, I started flicking through them and reading them. Then a photo fell out of one of them—somebody must have been using it as a bookmark years before. It was my mother in a wedding dress next to a tall, dark man in front of a church. And on the back in her handwriting it said, ''My marriage to Bill—5th July, 1965''.'

Josh looked thoughtful. 'Did you keep the picture?' he asked.

Penny made a face. 'I would have done,' she replied, 'but my mother came in while I was still looking at it and she just exploded. She snatched it out of my hands, ran upstairs and flung it in the fire.'

Josh whistled silently. 'Wow!' he said. 'Is she always like that?'

Penny smiled affectionately.

'No,' she replied. 'She's usually very calm and sensible. She's a librarian.'

His piercing green eyes held hers.

'Well, if she hated your dad so much, what did she have to say when you just up and left Australia to come here?' he asked. 'Didn't she try to talk you out of it?'

Penny pulled a face.

'I think she would have done,' she admitted candidly. 'But she wasn't there when the letter came from the lawyer. She was away in Europe on long-service leave from her job, and it just seemed like an opportunity too good to miss. For years I'd been dreaming about my father, wondering what he was like, wishing I could meet him. Somehow I've always felt sure that he was a really special kind of man. Of course, I was devastated to find out that he was dead, but it only made me feel even more strongly that I wanted to come here and find out about my American roots. Besides, I'd just reached a turning point in my life where I needed to take a break and get a fresh view of things, so coming to America seemed a good way to do it. And anyway, I'd never had a real adventure before in my entire life!'

'So you decided you'd just go wild and break out, huh?' asked Josh with a gleam of sympathetic mischief in his eyes. 'Well, good for you. So tell me about this property in Williamsburg County. You say your father died suddenly and left it to you?'

Penny bit her lip and nodded. It was a moment before she trusted herself to speak.

'Yes,' she agreed huskily. 'And that really meant a lot to me. Until then I was never sure whether he even knew or cared that I existed. But he cared enough to leave me something...'

Her brown eyes were soft and wistful and far away. Only when Josh's deep voice broke the silence did she jerk back to the present.

'Maybe,' said Josh cynically. 'But he didn't care enough to write to you all those years, did he?'

She glared at him.

'Why do you have to be so hateful?' she demanded. 'Maybe he did write and the letters got lost. Or maybe he didn't know where I lived. It's easy enough for you—anyone can see that you've been privileged from the moment you were born. Your family has probably lived in this house for the past two centuries. But I always felt as if I were nobody and belonged nowhere. So why do you have to spoil things for me now that I've finally found I have some roots after all?'

Josh winced at her heated tone. Then he raised both hands placatingly.

'As a matter of fact, my family hasn't been in this house for the last two centuries,' he said levelly. 'I bought it myself ten years ago and I've worked mighty hard for everything that's in it. But I take your point. I'm sorry if I offended you in what I said about your father. I never knew the man, so I'm hardly in a position to judge him.'

Penny was left feeling rather foolish.

'That's all right,' she muttered ungraciously. 'And you've really been very kind. But it's high time I stopped trespassing on your hospitality and moved into my own place. If you can just help me read the map, I'll go there this afternoon.'

Josh gave an exasperated snort.

'You are not trespassing,' he growled. 'All right, maybe I was a bit short with you last night. Well, that's because you were a darned nuisance. I had cotton sowing to organise today, and that don't wait for anybody. But that's all sorted out now, and you're welcome to stay here as long as you want. You're going to need help with that ankle—and besides...' He paused.

'And besides?' prompted Penny.

'I kind of like your company,' finished Josh offhandedly.

She flushed. She tried to keep her eyes fixed on the table, but felt them drawn insistently up to meet Josh's clear green eyes. Hours seemed to pass by as they sat looking at each other, and Penny felt as if all her senses were sharpened unbearably. She was acutely conscious of the distant ticking of a grandfather clock, the spicy aroma of the apple pie in its Pyrex dish, the starched stiffness of the tablecloth beneath her wrist. And more than anything else, she was conscious of Josh Miller. His hair was damp and tangled and his body was burnt almost to the colour of mahogany by the sun. In his faded Levi jeans and the open-necked shirt, he looked more like a pirate than ever. Never mind the carefully trimmed fingernails, the tangy odour of French after-shave, the elegant setting that surrounded him. This man was as raw and primitive as the earth he cultivated. And right now his eyes were undressing Penny with a sensuality that unnerved her.

'Th-thank you,' she stammered, looking hastily away. 'I like your company too, but I really must be going soon, because——'

His powerful brown fingers closed ruthlessly over hers.

'Don't,' he growled.

'Don't what?' fluttered Penny.

'Don't babble on like that. I don't want to listen to some stupid social small talk. All I want is the truth.'

She swallowed convulsively.

'I don't know what you mean,' she said huskily.

'Oh, yes, you do,' insisted Josh, and his fingers tightened on hers. 'There was something really special between us last night. Wasn't there?'

Penny snatched her hand out of his and looked away hastily.

'No!' she retorted through clenched teeth.

His fingers caught her under the chin and forced her to look at him. He was so close that she could see the fine lines around his narrowed green eyes and hear his rapid, uneven breathing.

'Are you telling me you kiss every man you meet like that?' he demanded brutally. 'Do you fall into the arms of every stranger as if he were the one man on earth you wanted to go to bed with?'

'No, of course I don't!' hissed Penny. 'How dare you say such a thing?'

Josh gave a mirthless laugh and drew the long cable of her corn-coloured hair towards him. Then he brushed it sensually across his lips and inhaled its fragrance.

'Well, if you don't,' he murmured hoarsely, 'I think you ought to admit that you and I had something pretty special going last night.'

Penny's heart seemed to be beating in the strangest fashion. She felt as if she were standing trapped on the railway tracks with an express train bearing down on her at high speed. Josh was watching her with naked desire in his eyes, and instead of feeling outraged she found her breath coming faster and her body arching as if to meet his. This time she did not have the excuse of exhaustion or medication. Yet to her dismay she found that a slow, pulsing warmth was spreading through every part of her. Horrified, she snatched her plaited hair away from him and fought back.

'Yes, of course,' she said coldly. 'If you call it special to try and seduce somebody who's half asleep and drugged into the bargain.'

Josh's chin came up and his eyes shot fire, as if she had slapped him. Springing to his feet, he strode angrily across the room and paused in front of the gilt mirror, with his hands clenched.

'I did not try to seduce you!' he snarled. 'Believe me, you wouldn't be sitting here untouched if I had. But I'm not low enough to take advantage of a girl who really doesn't know what she's doing. I prefer my women ready, willing and able!'

'Like Brenda Sue Hartley?' taunted Penny.

He swung round, his features rigid with shock.

'Who told you about Brenda Sue Hartley?' he demanded.

Penny flinched, but faced him defiantly.

'Mrs Cox at the hospital,' she retorted.

Josh's eyes were as bright and fierce as laser beams.

'What did she say?' he insisted.

'That Brenda Sue had got you leg-roped before you knew what was happening and that you were fixing to marry real soon,' replied Penny with a touch of malice.

Josh swore softly.

'Darned small town gossip!' he muttered. 'When I'm ready to marry, I'll do my own proposing, and I won't ask Wilma Cox to hang around with a megaphone to help me out.'

'Isn't it true, then?' asked Penny in a carefully casual voice.

For some reason, Josh's answer seemed terribly important. She sat forward in her seat, pleating the napkin between her fingers as she waited for him to reply. His eyes shifted under her intent gaze and he gave a small, uncomfortable shrug.

'True enough,' he admitted. 'At least, things were heading that way.'

'I see,' she said in a small, tight voice. She crumpled her napkin fiercely and set it down next to her plate. 'Then there's nothing more to be said, is there?'

Josh strode back across the room.

'Isn't there?' he challenged.

To Penny's dismay, he dropped on one knee and rested his arms on the back of her chair. She was uncomfortably conscious of his nearness. His hand brushed against her shoulder and she recoiled as if she had been stung. But his piercing green eyes held hers.

'Brenda Sue still dates other men,' he remarked conversationally. 'And I'd kind of like to give her a dose of her own medicine.'

'I am not a prescription drug!' pointed out Penny tartly.

He laughed and ruffled the top of her hair.

'No, but you're sassy and opinionated, and I'd really like to get to know you,' he replied. 'Why don't you stay on a while so I can show you around the place? There's a lot we could do, even with your ankle strapped up. Horse and buggy rides around Charleston, cruising on the harbour, trips to Myrtle Beach. I could even rent a wheelchair and take you around the shopping malls, if you like. What do you say?'

Penny shrugged impatiently.

'What's the point, Josh?' she demanded. 'I'm not interested in casual affairs, I never have been. And how could this be anything else? You're involved with Brenda Sue and I'm going back to Australia in less than a month. We'd be fools even to think of it.'

'We could just do it as friends,' suggested Josh.

His gaze lingered for a moment on the gentle swell of her breasts and then darted hastily away.

'Could we?' retorted Penny sceptically.

'No,' he admitted gloomily.

He rose to his feet and stood gazing down at her.

'Well, if you must go,' he said with a sigh, 'I guess I'd better drive you to your father's house and make sure the place is still fit for you to stay in. Do you have the address?'

Penny took a folded sketch map out of her pocket and spread it out on the table.

'It must be quite close to here,' she said, frowning thoughtfully. 'But unfortunately none of these back country roads seem to have the names posted on them. It's about a mile off Clarksville Road and it's called Merivale.'

'Merivale?' Josh stared at her aghast, his features suddenly rigid with shock. 'Are you sure?'

'Yes, it's right here on the map that the lawyer sent. See? Josh, what's wrong?'

For Josh was staring down at the map with his lips pursed in an incredulous gasp.

'Merivale?' he repeated, stunned. 'There have never been any Owens at Merivale. That fool lawyer must have messed up good.'

'Don't get so steamed up, Josh!' begged Penny. 'The lawyer didn't mess up. It's just that my surname is different from my father's. You see, my mother changed back to her maiden name when she was divorced and I've always used it too. My father's name was different.'

The dining-room suddenly seemed cold and chill. In the silence that followed, Penny was intensely conscious of the whispering sweep of the ceiling fans and the shrilling of katydids outside the french windows. Josh spoke and, when he did, his voice was as cool and neutral as if they were meeting for the first time.

'So what was your father's name?' he demanded.

'Eliot,' replied Penny clearly. 'William C. Eliot.'

'What?'

Penny flinched as Josh slammed his hand down on the dining table, setting the plates rattling.

'W-what's wrong?' she whispered.

'Eliot,' repeated Josh. 'You're William C. Eliot's daughter?'

She nodded slowly. 'Did you know him?' she asked.

'Yes,' he said curtly.

The sudden radiance on her face was like sunlight after a storm. Putting out her hand, she touched Josh's arm.

'What was he like?' she asked eagerly.

He turned away, gritting his teeth.

'Didn't you like him?' faltered Penny, dropping her hand.

He opened his mouth and then looked at the wistful, half-apprehensive expression on her face. He grimaced.

'No, I can't say I did,' he admitted. 'But it was nothing important, and a lot of people around these parts thought he was a fine man. It just came as kind of a shock to me, hearing that it was Merivale you'd inherited. Didn't you say something about staying in the place while you're here?'

Penny nodded, her eyes shining. Then slowly her face puckered into an expression of dismay.

'What is it?' she asked. 'Is something wrong? Have vandals smashed the windows or something?'

'Worse than that,' replied Josh heavily. 'I'm sorry, Penny, but there's something you should know about Merivale.'

'What?' she cried, starting halfway to her feet. 'What should I know?'

'It's burnt to the ground,' explained Josh bluntly. 'Didn't the lawyer tell you?'

She gasped.

'But when did it burn? Did my father——?'

'Your father died in the fire,' cut in Josh grimly.

'Dear God!' breathed Penny. Her face turned deathly pale and she swayed in her seat.

The next few minutes were a jumbled blur. When she finally gained control of herself, she found Josh was dabbing her eyes with a table napkin and holding a glass of iced water to her lips.

'I'm sorry,' she said in a dazed voice. 'It was just such a shock. I really had no idea——'

'Look,' urged Josh, setting down the iced water and retreating to his place at the end of the table, 'you don't have to put yourself through all this, Penny. You told me before that you wanted to sell the place. Well, it

borders my property and I'll give you a fair price for it.
You won't even need to go look at it, because——'

'No!' she cut in.

She found that her teeth were chattering on the rim
of the glass and she set it down very slowly and delib-
erately, trying to ignore the shaking of her hands.

'I want to see it, Josh. I want to see where my father
lived, however awful it is. Nobody has the right to de-
prive me of that. And I didn't come all this way just to
climb on a plane and go back home without ever setting
foot on my own property.'

Josh was silent for a moment, but his jaw was set
grimly. A muscle twitched in his cheek.

'All right,' he agreed levelly. 'You get your crutches
and I'll drive you out there. Then, when you've seen
enough, I'll take you to a motel.'

He was no longer trying to persuade her to stay at
Waterford Hall, Penny noticed. In fact, he wore the distinct air of a man trying to get a distasteful duty over
with as fast as possible. Striding across the room, he
held the door open for her, but did not even glance down
at her as she limped awkwardly into the hall. And on
the short drive to Merivale, his face remained guarded
and expressionless.

To Penny's surprise, he did not take the car out on
to the public highway, but instead chose a sandy track
which wound away out of sight behind Waterford Hall.
This unexpected back road looped around the old
smokehouse and brick slave cabins at the rear of the
main building, then led across a wooden bridge spanning
a marshy backwater. Through the open window Penny
heard the shrilling of katydids and the splash and ripple
of waterfowls among the high green reeds.

'It's really wild country, isn't it?' she said tentatively.
'So lush and green and steamy.'

'Roll your window up,' ordered Josh rudely. 'The air-
conditioning doesn't work when it's open.'

She was taken aback by this surly response, but she
had no time to brood over it, for, as the car rounded
the next bend, she caught her first glimpse of Merivale.
It must once have been an enchanting spot for a house.
In this wide loop of the river, the reeds gave way to a
vast sweep of cool green water and on its very edge a
boatshed and jetty were still standing. Fifty yards away
on a low rise, half a dozen live oaks marked out the
boundaries of the house site. Brick paths still ran in her-
ringbone patterns around the remains of a colourful
flower garden, but the beds were choked with weeds.
And the only relic of any dwelling was a single charred
and ramshackle chimney. Penny took a long irregular
breath.

'Do you want to get out and take a look?' asked Josh
tersely, guiding the car to a halt on a stretch of broken
brick paving.

'Yes,' she agreed.

She scarcely noticed his harsh tone, being too preoccupied with her own uprush of emotion. Her father
had lived here. Up until a year ago, he had walked along
these paths, tended these flowers, looked out on this
view. And then died tragically on this spot. The thought
made her throat swell, and swinging her crutches determinedly, she made her way around the brick paths until
she had criss-crossed every inch of the place. At last she
limped slowly back to Josh, brimming with the need to
share her feelings. She had already witnessed the
powerful bond that tied Josh to this country. If anyone
could understand how she felt, he would.

'Well,' he growled, as she came to a halt. 'Are you
prepared to sell?'

The bluntness of it took Penny's breath away. She had
come to Josh expecting sympathy and understanding.
Instead he was behaving like the worst kind of real estate
shark. Her mouth tightened.

'Give me one good reason why I should,' she
challenged.

He shrugged, as if it were a matter of no importance to him. For some reason this only infuriated her more.

'The house is gone,' he pointed out. 'And without it the land is practically worthless. I doubt if anybody else would want to buy it, but I'm prepared to take it off your hands. It was part of the Waterford Hall estate years ago and I'd kind of like to see it all reunited. Let's say twenty thousand dollars.'

As he spoke, he reached into the back pocket of his jeans and drew out his cheque book. The casual certainty of this action made Penny's annoyance boil over.

'No,' she snapped.

'What do you mean?' demanded Josh incredulously. 'It's a good price, the best you'll ever get.'

'That's a shame,' retorted Penny, 'because the place is not for sale.'

'But you told me yesterday you were going to sell.'

'I've changed my mind.'

Josh gave an exasperated snort.

'I suppose that means that you want more money for it,' he sneered. 'All right—twenty-five thousand.'

'It's—not—for—sale,' repeated Penny very slowly and loudly. 'Don't you understand English?'

Josh's face hardened.

'Maybe not, but I understand plain greed when I see it,' he snarled. 'And let me tell you, Miss Owen, you make some of those Californian property developers look like innocent babies. Just as a matter of interest, what price would you sell this place for?'

For a moment, she felt an overpowering urge to pick up one of her crutches and hit him with it. But then an even more satisfying reaction occurred to her. She gave him a long, slow calculating look.

'A hundred thousand dollars,' she replied sweetly.

Josh drew in a breath.

'You're crazy!' he snapped. 'But I might have known William Eliot's daughter would try to pull a stunt like that. Well, I'm sorry, honey, but I'm just not playing your tricky little games. You'll sell to me in time, but by heaven, it'll be on my terms, not yours!'

Blazing green eyes met stony brown ones.

'How can you be so sure?' taunted Penny.

'What choice do you have?' he demanded. 'I can tell you now, nobody else will want this place, and you need to sell, ma'am. You've got to be back in Australia in less than a month!'

He had her backed into a corner and she knew it, but some inner core of stubbornness would not allow her to surrender so easily. Tossing her head defiantly, she made the silliest statement she had ever made in her life.

'That's where you're wrong, Mr Miller,' she purred. 'Because I'm not going back to Australia. I'm staying put right here!'

CHAPTER THREE

'YOU'RE going to live here in South Carolina?' exclaimed Sarah McKendrick in surprise. 'Well, my land, that's just wonderful! But where you going to stay, honey? That old Merivale place ain't worth a toot now, and that's the truth!'

'I know,' agreed Penny ruefully, biting her lip.

She was beginning to regret the rash impulse that had led her to make the announcement in the first place, but at least its effect on Josh had been wholly satisfactory. After a single growl of outrage, he had bundled her into the car, driven back to Waterford Hall at a reckless, jolting pace and promptly thrust her into the arms of Sarah McKendrick. Then, with a brief, smouldering glance, he had announced that he had work to do and marched out, slamming the kitchen door behind him. Penny's triumph was complete. Unfortunately it was also short-lived. Thinking about the difficulties of resigning from her job in Sydney, putting a roof over her head and even getting back to Kingswood Hospital for a checkup on her ankle made her quail. But pride would not allow her to back down.

'There must be some way I could stay at Merivale,' she said despairingly.

Sarah paused in her energetic whisking of a chocolate chip cookie mix and looked thoughtful.

'How about one of them mobile homes?' she suggested. 'Now they're real comfortable. They're just as big as a regular house at only a fraction of the cost. I believe you could buy one of those new for about twenty thousand dollars. Or you might get a used one for a lot less.'

Penny did a rapid calculation. The legacy from her father had included some money, but she was reluctant to splurge it all just for the pleasure of upsetting Josh Miller.

'It would have to be second-hand,' she said doubtfully. 'But I suppose it would take ages to buy one and set it up.'

'I don't know about that,' replied Sarah briskly, ladling cookie mix out on to the baking trays. 'They're advertised most every day in the newspaper, and it wouldn't be much trouble to put one up on that site. Of course, they might have to run new electricity wires in, but the cesspool would already be there. Why, I believe you could get it all set up in less than a week.'

'A week?' mused Penny slowly. 'You know, it really sounds tempting, Mrs McKendrick.'

'And my sister-in-law, Lilian Brown, would be glad to put you up for a while, until your own home was ready,' continued Sarah persuasively. 'She doesn't live but half a mile down the road from Merivale and she's been real lonely since my brother did. Why, if you really want to do this, Miss Penny, we can have you sorted out in no time!'

Sarah McKendrick was as good as her word, and the result was that ten days later Penny stood in the living-room of her mobile home and watched as the electrician emerged from the crawl-space underneath. He dusted off his hands and closed the trapdoor, then walked across the room and flicked a light switch.

'Well, there you go!' he said. 'Everything in working order, ma'am. Now you got nothing to do except wait for your first visitor.'

'But you haven't checked everything,' protested Penny. 'Couldn't you just try the rest of the power points to make sure everything's working?'

'Don't have time right now,' replied the electrician, stuffing a wad of gum into his mouth. 'I gotta house call to make down the road a ways. But I'll call in later.'

As the man's pick-up truck bumped away down the sandy drive, Penny walked slowly inside and set the coffee percolator on her sparkling new stove. Then, sitting down at her pine dining-table, she rested her chin in her hands and sighed.

'Oh, help, what have I done?' she groaned.

It was exciting to own her very first home, but somehow terrifying too. At least in these circumstances. Like any girl, she had occasionally daydreamed of the day when she would marry and set up house. But the daydreams inevitably involved a happy whirlwind of shopping as part of a couple, not this bittersweet pilgrimage around shopping malls and hardware stores entirely on her own. Well, not entirely alone. Sarah McKendrick and her friends and relations had considered it their bounden duty to offer a little neighbourly help to get Penny set up. And neighbourly help in these parts covered everything from driving her to the doctor to bringing over batches of hot biscuits and fried chicken 'in case her ankle wasn't up to cooking'. Penny's lips curved in a reminiscent smile as she thought about it. Southern hospitality was overwhelming, and her new freezer held more food than she could possibly eat in a year. And there had been invitations galore to parties and dinners and barbecues. Yet every night she lay awake listening to the lonely whistle of distant trains and worrying herself sick about the same problem. Was this the most reckless, spendthrift action she had ever taken in her life?

The volcanic bubbling of the coffee percolator interrupted her thoughts, and she limped across to the stove. Turning the knob to switch it off, she frowned anxiously up at the range hood and ventilator fan. Was it her imagination, or did the fan sound strange? She was still frowning at it thoughtfully when she heard the sound of confident footsteps striding across the porch and the squeak of the screen door. With a sigh of relief she turned round, expecting the electrician.

'I'm so glad you've come back,' she began. 'I think the fan... Oh!'

For it was not the electrician who stood there, but the man she wanted least to see in the whole world. Josh Miller. He smiled sardonically.

'Well, go on, honey,' he begged. 'You're so glad I've come back and you think the fan has... what? Died of natural causes? Seen fifty years' service in a hamburger joint before it was installed in your kitchen? Been inadvertently switched with the propeller on a motorboat? Hell, it sure sounds like it!'

Penny winced.

'I didn't know it was you,' she pointed out unnecessarily. 'I thought it was the electrician coming back to check that everything worked. He said he would.'

Josh picked up a carton with a large sticker on its side saying 'BUCKMEISTER'S FOR QUALITY ELECTRICAL GOODS AND SERVICE' and sniffed sardonically.

'Hank Buckmeister?' he sniffed incredulously. 'You must be joking, sugar. That guy won't be round for months if you've paid him already. Have you?'

Penny bit her lip and nodded miserably. Josh gave an exasperated sigh.

'Well, I used to service aircraft fifteen years ago when I was in the Air Force,' he said. 'I guess it can't be all that different. I'll take a look at it for you.'

Before she could even open her mouth to protest, he had sprung lightly up on to the counter top, switched off the offending fan and was forcefully levering the metal grille out of the range hood.

'Look, there's no need——' began Penny, but he ignored her.

'Do you have a crescent wrench?' he demanded.

'A crescent... ?' Penny looked blank.

'What you'd call a spanner,' he retorted, still peering intently into the hood. 'Oh, forget it. I'll get my tool kit out of my four-wheel-drive—it'll be faster.'

He was across the room in four strides and out of the door before Penny had a chance to argue. Before long he was back, carrying a toolkit. Holding the heavy box casually in one hand, he reached out his other arm and flipped a switch at the mains to turn off the power. But this time Penny was not going to be so easily overruled. Planting herself firmly in front of the stove, she blocked his path.

'Josh,' she said in a low, tense voice, 'I appreciate your concern, but this is my house, and there is absolutely no need for you to mess about with the wiring. In fact, I absolutely forbid you to do so!'

He sighed audibly. Setting down the toolbox, he picked up Penny instead and deposited her bodily in one of the dining chairs.

'Pour me a cup of coffee, will you, honey?' he demanded. 'This won't take but a minute.'

To her overpowering rage and humiliation, this prediction proved almost exactly correct. In point of fact it was two and a half minutes before Josh gave a shout of triumph, leapt to the floor, switched on the electricity and then turned on the fan. It sprang into life with an efficient purring sound that was totally different from its earlier racket.

'Easy!' he exclaimed, wiping his hands on Penny's best tea-towel. 'Now, where's my coffee?'

She glared at him.

'Well, come on,' he urged. 'I fixed your fan. Least you can do is offer me a cup of coffee.'

'I didn't ask you to fix it,' she pointed out acidly.

He grinned infuriatingly.

'Hell, I know that,' he agreed amiably. 'You're so damned stiffnecked you wouldn't ask for a lifebelt if you were drowning. But now that it's done, I figure you owe me something for it.'

Penny gritted her teeth.

'Let me pay you for it,' she suggested.

Josh's eyes met hers, green and taunting and full of challenge.

'Oh, no, honey,' he said softly. 'There are some things that can't be bought, and neighbourliness is one of them.'

Penny tossed her head. It galled her to think of being under an obligation to this man, but there seemed to be no way out. Pursing her lips, she poured a cup of coffee and set it down wordlessly on the dining-table.

'Aren't you going to join me?' demanded Josh.

As warily as if she were going to a tea-party with a rattlesnake, she filled her own cup and sat down opposite him. He took a slow, enjoyable draught of coffee and looked at her keenly.

'You're off your crutches,' he commented. 'That's good. How long does the doctor figure it will be before your ankle is back to normal?'

'A few weeks,' said Penny, relieved that the topic was such a neutral one. Although she had chosen a chair as far away as possible from Josh, the sight of his muscular bronzed figure seemed to be causing a strange disturbance in her breathing. 'I have...I have an elastic bandage. And a walking stick. And people around here have been awfully kind, driving me around and giving me things. Lilian Brown gave me that rocking chair over there. She said it had been in her attic for twenty years and she figured somebody ought to get some use out of it.'

Josh's gaze roved admiringly round the room, taking in the blue and white checked curtains at the windows, the rocking chair with its floral cushion, the comfortable but slightly frayed sofa and the blue rag rug on the board floor.

'The place looks real nice,' he said sincerely. 'You've done a mighty fine job in ten days, especially seeing that you weren't so mobile.'

Penny warmed to him.

'Thanks,' she replied, flashing him a cautious smile. And then he ruined everything.

'Of course, you really ought to have a man around the place,' he remarked with the air of somebody stating the obvious. 'You sure aren't up to running things on your own.'

She took a deep breath and counted up to ten. Then she let out a strangled groan. He looked at her in mild surprise.

'What's the matter?' he asked. 'Didn't the coffee agree with you?'

'The coffee was fine!' raged Penny, jumping to her feet. 'You're the one who doesn't agree with me, with your stupid, antiquated male chauvinist ideas! Just because I'm a female and you were evidently born before World War One, you think I'm totally useless! You think I can't even turn on a stove by myself or cross a road or open a can. You probably think I can't even breathe without help! So why didn't you bring me an iron lung out of your damned four-wheel-drive while you were at it?'

She paused for breath, and he watched her with a glint of amusement in his narrowed green eyes.

'I would have done if I'd known you wanted it,' he murmured provocatively.

Penny let out an angry wail.

'You're insufferable!' she stormed, waving her arms in frantic circles. 'You don't think I'm any use for anything, do you?'

She turned away, and stumbled over the empty carton. Suddenly Josh was beside her, his strong arms saving her from a possible fall.

'Yes, I do, honey,' he crooned, holding her against him. 'Of course I do.'

'Well, what?' she demanded in a voice that threatened tears. 'What am I good for?'

Josh's heart was beating violently through his thin T-shirt. She could feel the hard muscular outline of his chest against her body, and, as she tried to twist out of his grip, the full, ripe curve of her breasts brushed against his arm. He caught his breath.

'You're good for this,' he murmured hoarsely.

Then, crushing her hard up against him, he kissed her full on the mouth. For the space of five heartbeats Penny felt as if she were suspended outside time, conscious only of a roaring in her ears, the frantic drumming of blood through every inch of her body and the warm demanding pressure of Josh's lips on hers. His fingers came up and traced a whorl on her left cheek, then moved slowly downwards and repeated the same movement on her breast. She let out a muffled gasp of longing and her body arched instinctively into his. The hard throbbing length of his masculine frame pressed against her, and tingling thrills of excitement coursed through every nerve in her body. Her mouth opened slowly and sensually under his, and she closed her eyes, leaning into him, so that his powerful arms held her as if she were dancing or floating on a cloud. Then at last her eyelashes fluttered open.

'I hate you,' she said weakly.

She felt rather than heard his throaty chuckle of amusement. Its vibration rippled through her entire body.

'Tell me that as if you mean it and maybe I'll believe you,' he replied huskily, still rubbing her nipples in slow circles of fire.

She drew away from him with a shudder of regret and folded her arms protectively across her body.

'You make me feel dehumanised,' she complained. 'You're not interested in me as a person, only as a sex object!'

'That's not true!' protested Josh. 'I didn't come here intending to make love to you. It just happened that way.'

'Well, why did you come here?' demanded Penny suspiciously. 'Last time we were together, you didn't seem to be enjoying my company all that much.'

He sat down and grinned reflectively.

'Hell, no!' he agreed. 'I was so burned up at your stupid darned stubbornness, all I wanted to do was wring your neck.'

'So that's what you've come back for, is it?' she asked tartly. 'To wring my neck?'

He touched her throat caressingly and chuckled.

'Don't tempt me, sweetheart,' he crooned. Then, hooking one of his long legs around a chair, he drew it to him and sat down. With an air of being completely at home, he poured himself more coffee. 'No, that's not what I came for. I came to see if you're ready to sell yet.'

'Ready to sell?' echoed Penny incredulously.

'Yep. Here, have some coffee. You don't look so good.'

She ground her teeth.

'Don't you offer me coffee in my own house!' she stormed.

'Suit yourself,' shrugged Josh. 'Mind now, I don't blame you for refusing. This is terrible coffee. You ought to ask for espresso grind when you're using that kind of percolator.'

She choked.

'If you've finished drinking my coffee, insulting my tastes, massaging my nipples and mending my fan, then I suggest you leave!' she shouted.

Josh smiled maddeningly.

'Not until we discuss my business proposal,' he reminded her.

'What proposal?' grated Penny.

'My proposal to buy you out.'

'We already discussed it ten days ago and I refused,' retorted Penny.

'Sure,' agreed Josh mildly. 'But you've had time to calm down a mite since then. You've had your fun, you've put up your mobile home and you've proved your point, whatever the hell that was. Don't you think it's

time you acted like a rational human being, instead of
a nursery school kid, and started talking sense?'

Penny fumed for a moment before replying.

'I am not acting like a nursery school kid!' she protested indignantly.

'Aren't you, honey?' demanded Josh. 'Well, you could
have fooled me. You've bought a mobile home, paid an
arm and a leg to a no-good electrician to wire it up for
you, wasted good money filling it with penny-annie furniture, and now you're fixing on giving up a good job
just so you can stay here. And what for? The only reason
I can think of is that you want to spite me.'

This was so close to the truth that for a moment Penny
was rendered speechless. She sank into a chair and glared
defiantly at him with her colour coming and going and
tears threatening dangerously.

'That's not true,' she breathed at last.

'Isn't it?' he murmured, reaching out absently and
tidying her braid back over her shoulder. 'I'd sure like
to believe you, Penny, but I just can't. Seems to me that
you're just plain reckless, and spendthrift into the
bargain. But it's still not too late to do something about
it. My earlier offer for the land still stands, and I'll even
take this gimcracky mobile home off your hands for
whatever price you paid for it. I won't pretend I really
want it, but I could always house one of my cotton-
pickers in it.'

'No!'

The violence of Penny's response astonished both of
them. A great tidal wave of indignation had swept
through her as she listened to Josh, and now it thundered around her like a gigantic breaker.

'I don't care what you're offering,' she hissed. 'I don't
care what you think my motives are or what your opinion
is of my character. My property is not for sale, and if
it were, you would be the last person I'd sell it to. Now
why don't you just pick up your box of tools and your
business proposals and get out of here?'

But Josh stood his ground with maddening nonchalance.

'And what exactly are you going to do if you stay on here?' he demanded. 'This isn't Sydney, Australia, it's a quiet little country backwater. You won't be able to find a job in advertising unless you go some place like Charleston, and that's fifty miles away. And even then you'd have to have a work permit, which isn't easy to get if you're a foreign citizen. So how do you think you're even going to support yourself?'

Penny tossed her head defiantly.

'It may interest you to know that I have dual Australian and American citizenship!' she retorted. 'So I don't need a work permit. And in any case, I still have enough money left from my inheritance to keep me going!'

Josh sneered.

'That's real smart!' he exclaimed. 'Living off your capital when you should be using it to get your career established. Like I said, Penny, you're just a nursery school kid. Why don't you do yourself a favour and grow up?'

'And why don't you do yourself a favour and mind your own business?' seethed Penny. 'I didn't ask for your advice and I didn't ask for your offer on my property. Now kindly get out!'

He shrugged and drank the last of his coffee. Then he looked straight into her eyes. She quailed inwardly at the disapproval in his scowling dark brows, his intent green eyes and his grimly set mouth, but somehow she managed to meet his gaze. And even gave him a saucy, provocative smile designed to infuriate him. His mouth hardened.

'Suit yourself,' he said in a voice soft with rage. 'But you haven't heard the last of me, ma'am. I'll be back here every week repeating my offer until I bring you to your knees—and that's a promise. Now good morning to you!'

* * *

Left alone, Penny covered her face with her hands and shuddered. I hate that man, she thought despairingly. I just hate him. Thrusting away her untouched coffee, she limped moodily across to the window and stared out at the river. The trouble was that, however much Josh infuriated her, he also excited her in a way that she had never imagined possible. His caresses left her body tingling and aching for fulfilment, but it was more than just that. Any woman would be attracted by Josh's raw animal magnetism, but that alone could not explain the effect he had on Penny. Even while she was spitting defiance at him, she was conscious of a blind, instinctive yearning to make him want her as badly as she wanted him. Nothing less would do. The realisation horrified her, especially since she had always prided herself on being cool and sensible and rational. Yet from the moment she had met Josh, another side of her character seemed to have come to life. A side that was passionate, impulsive and totally foolhardy. Penny clenched her fists in frustration on the windowsill and uttered a low groan. Although she would never in a million years admit it to Josh, the way she was behaving over this mobile home was quite ridiculous.

However much she tried to deny it, he really was right to criticise her. She *had* only bought the mobile home to annoy him, and her money *was* ebbing away at a frightening rate. He was even right about her lack of an occupation. So far she had been kept busy getting her house set up, but that would soon be in order and it wouldn't be long before boredom attacked her. If only she had something to do... The flash of an egret's flight caught her eye, and she watched appreciatively as the bird sailed down to a smooth landing on the wooden jetty. I'd love to paint that, she thought. The river flowing away like molten green glass and all that jungly green vegetation in the background, and then, right in the centre of the painting, the white egret preening its feathers... She stopped dead with an arrested ex-

pression on her face. Of course, she thought exultantly.
How blindingly, brilliantly simple! That's what I'll do
at Merivale. I'll paint!

The next time Lilian Brown drove into Charleston,
Penny accompanied her with her cheque-book and a
shopping list tucked safely into her bag. She explored
every art supply store in the city, and finally arrived home
exhausted and triumphant at ten o'clock at night with
Lilian's car piled high with sketch-pads, an easel, tur-
pentine and tubes of paint. And for the next month she
spent almost every waking hour hard at work. On fine
days she set up her easel in the shade of one of the huge
live oak trees and did her best to ignore the biting gnats
and the steamy heat. When the sky split open and rain
poured down in torrents, she moved into the spare
bedroom and happily filled in details or cleaned her
brushes. And once a week she changed out of her paint-
stained shorts and T-shirt into a clean summer dress for
the pleasure of slamming the door in Josh Miller's face.

It was on the Monday morning following one of these
encounters that Penny came to a momentous decision.
In spite of her decisive façade whenever she met Josh,
her own misgivings about staying on in America had
always continued to gnaw at her. At the back of her
mind she had always known that she could still put
Merivale up for sale and slink back to her job in Sydney.
But now she had reached the point of no return. Her
holiday leave was almost over, and in common decency
she would have to resign from her job if she intended
to stay on. Not only that, but she would have to write
to her mother. With a sinking feeling as if she were going
to the dentist, Penny sat down at the kitchen table and
picked up a writing pad.

The note of resignation was straightforward enough,
but the letter to her mother caused several crumpled
sheets of paper to be thrown impatiently on the floor
before she was satisfied. Although Penny and her mother
were deeply attached to each other, they had quite dif-

ferent temperaments, and the last six months had seen
increasing clashes between them. The last and worst of
these had sprung from Penny's decision to end her engagement to Simon, and Penny was still smarting over
her mother's disapproval. Not that it had ever come to
outright quarrelling between them—they were far too
fond of each other for that. But Caroline Owen had made
her misgivings plainly apparent right up until the moment
when she had left for her European holiday.

Penny winced as she recalled the scene at Sydney
airport. Of course there was nothing dramatic about it;
her mother was far too quiet and well-mannered for that.
But as Caroline Owen put her hands on her daughter's
shoulders and kissed her cheek before boarding her
plane, she let slip a remark that had rankled ever since.
'Oh, Penny, I do hope you know what you're doing
about poor Simon. I'm afraid you're going to regret
being so impetuous!' Not a very serious criticism, certainly not the sort of thing that started family vendettas.
Yet it had been enough to make Penny miserably uncomfortable about her own decision. Was she crying for
the moon? Was she a fool to throw over a man who was
everything her mother claimed? Financially secure, re-
liable, a good provider. True, he was pompous, had no
sense of humour and Penny wasn't in love with him, but
according to her mother none of that mattered. Penny
had returned home from the airport with a heavy heart,
feeling as if her life was in chaos all because of her own
nebulous yearning for freedom and adventure.

It was while she was still in this state of turmoil that
the letter about her father's death reached her. At once
all the vague dreams of her childhood came surging back,
and she was struck by an overwhelming impulse to travel
to America and lay some old, tormenting ghosts. Half
seduced by this tantalising prospect, she had gone into
her mother's room and rummaged through Caroline's
desk in search of her passport. And there she had come
upon some documents which had left her reeling with

shock. Neatly filed letters and forms which proved that her mother had registered her in babyhood as an American citizen. And yet Penny had never even been told about it. Why? What mystery was there about her American background that must never be revealed? Surprise and resentment welled up inside her, along with a fierce determination to learn the truth. It was as much that discovery as anything else which had sent her winging her way to America and plunged her into the events of the last few weeks. And now she was faced with the complex task of explaining her decision to her mother.

Anger and bewilderment surged through her as she stared down at the writing pad. She felt outraged and hurt by her mother's secretive decision to keep her in the dark about her American citizenship. And yet trying to explain her feelings was impossible. The only way she had ever been able to express the passionate intensity of her inner self was in her painting. In every other aspect of her life, she had always been Caroline Owen's daughter, sensible, calm and rational. But now she felt as if that façade was cracking dangerously and a new Penny was beginning to emerge, a woman who was vibrantly certain of the rightness of kicking over the traces and starting a whole new life in America. A woman who could be crazy enough to set herself up as an artist in the backblocks of South Carolina and know that she was doing the right thing. But it wasn't easy to explain any of that to her mother, particularly the part that Josh Miller played in her decision. In the end she decided to gloss over the complicated details of the mobile home and her encounter with Josh. Chewing her Biro, she looked down at what she had written.

Dear Mum,

I'm writing to tell you some really extraordinary news. Just after you left for Europe, I had a letter from a lawyer in South Carolina, saying that my father had died and left me some property here—a house and ten acres. I felt I just had to come and see the place, so here I am! What's more, I'm resigning from my job in Sydney and I'm going to stay here, at least for a year or so. I always wanted a chance to try and be a genuine artist instead of a commercial one, and I guess this is it.

I know it's not the kind of decision you would approve of. Not cautious or responsible or any of those things that you always wanted me to be, but which I don't think I am, deep down. Yet it's what I want to do more than anything else in the world. You never would talk about my father, and that always made me feel an awful sense of loss. Well, now that I'm finally here in America, I feel whole again. And, perhaps once I'm settled in, I can find out more about my father and really put down roots here.

There's something else you should know. Just before I left, I was looking for my passport in your desk. I found it in the end, but what I found first was the certificate of my American citizenship. It came as a terrible shock to me. I can't imagine why you applied for it on my behalf and then never told me about it. I suppose you thought having dual citizenship would be useful to me, but why didn't you tell me? My father had to sign the papers for it, so you must have been in touch with him at least once after he left, although you always let me assume you didn't even know where he lived. Please, Mum, don't you think it's time you told me the truth about what happened between you? I realise that he must have hurt you in some way, perhaps by going off with another woman, but whatever he did, he was my father. So surely I have a right to know?

I hope you won't feel that I'm being disloyal to you in what I've written or what I've chosen to do. After all, I'm twenty-four now and it is my life. But please believe that I'm always,

Your loving daughter,

Penny.

P.S. All the people here are really nice, except for my next-door neighbour, Josh Miller. Just because he's wealthy and good-looking, he thinks he can roll right over people and tell them what to do. I can't stand him.

When she had finished the final draft, Penny read it through slowly two or three times and then folded it carefully and put it in an envelope.

'Well, this is it!' she said to her reflection in the mirror by the front door. 'I've really burnt my boats now.'

Yet oddly enough, as she locked the door and set out for the post office, she did not feel in the least bit apprehensive. Instead a giddy, bubbling feeling of exhilaration overtook her. The air was warm and soft and moist, the river was green and still and the katydids were shrilling a loud chorus as she marched purposefully along the track that led to Waterford Hall. It felt good to be alive, and she laughed aloud for sheer delight as she saw the avenue of crepe myrtles that led to the back entrance of the big house. White and lilac and watermelon-pink, they looked like a troupe of ballet dancers intermingled with the drabber colours of the dogwoods. But the dogwoods too would have their season, she thought with satisfaction. And she would still be here next springtime when they bloomed. Hesitantly she reached out and touched the rough grey bark of one of the trees, trying to imagine it covered in shimmering white flowers. It was a pity she was on such bad terms with Josh Miller, otherwise she could have asked his advice about setting up a garden of her own. As it was, she didn't even want him to see her taking a short cut to the post office over his land. Glancing uneasily over her shoulder, she headed determinedly for the public road.

Twenty minutes later she arrived in the tiny village of Clarksville. The postmistress, a plump, grey-haired woman with permed hair and large red plastic earrings, looked up with a friendly smile as Penny opened the door.

'Well, hello there,' she said, setting down her crossword puzzle. 'I'll just bet you're the Australian girl that's moved into the Merivale property down the road. Ain't that right?'

'Yes,' agreed Penny with an embarrassed smile.

'Welcome to Williamsburg County,' continued the woman. 'I'm Betty Anne Summers. And what's your name, honey?'

'Penny Owen,' replied Penny, setting her letters on the counter.

'Owen,' mused Betty Anne. 'Yes, I believe Wilma Cox told me that. Now what can I do to help you, Miss Penny?'

'I need some airmail stamps for these letters, please,' replied Penny.

Betty Anne lifted her spectacles from their chain around her neck and frowned down at the envelopes. Her lips moved as she scanned the addresses.

'Gleeson's Advertising Agency, Sydney, Australia. That'll be forty-five cents. And what's this one? Ms. C. S. Owen, Poste Restante, Lisbon, Portugal. Is that a relative of yours, honey?'

'Yes,' agreed Penny, wriggling slightly at this inquisition. 'My mother.'

'Oh, my land! Portugal! Whatever's she doin' there?'

Penny began to feel that a visit to the dentist might have been preferable. At least the extractions would have been quicker.

'She's on holiday,' she replied. 'Three months' long-service leave. She's touring around Europe.'

Betty Anne gave a satisfied nod and stuck a stamp on each of the airmail envelopes.

'You fixin' on stayin' long in these parts?' she asked curiously. 'I guess you must be if you bought a house here.'

Penny surrendered.

'Yes, I'm giving up my job in Sydney,' she admitted. 'So I'll probably be staying on here for a while.'

'Well, ain't that something?' exclaimed Betty Anne. 'Well, you'll be real welcome, honey. Besides, it's nice to think somebody's living in that Merivale place again. Why, it was just tragic when the old house burned down, especially with Mr William and his mama inside it! He was the cutest man, good-lookin' and full of charm.'

'Really?' asked Penny with a quickening of interest. 'He was my father, you know.'

'Oo-ee! Is that right?' gasped Mrs Summers, laying one hand to her ample bosom. 'Well, I declare, that is about the saddest thing I ever heard of. To think of you losing your daddy and your grandmama both at the same time!'

Penny bit her lip. She really didn't want to discuss her deepest feelings about her father with a total stranger, but she was also hungry for any crumbs of information about him.

'Yes, it was sad,' she agreed levelly. 'But I never met him, so I don't feel it as badly as if we'd been really close. Did you know him well, Mrs Summers?'

'No, I cain't say as I did,' admitted Betty Anne, leaning her meaty forearms comfortably on the counter and settling down for a good gossip. 'I believe he spent most of his life goin' backwards and forwards to foreign parts, and he only came back here to live within his mama about two years ago. He'd had some kind of business problems and lost a whole bunch of money. That was a real pity, mind, because the Eliots used to be mighty important folks in these parts. Why, your grandaddy used to own that big house at Waterford Hall and over three thousand acres of prime farmland back in the old days. And that all came to your daddy on his twenty-first birthday.'

'Waterford Hall?' exclaimed Penny, aghast. 'You mean . . . Josh Miller's house? It belonged to my father?'

'Yes, ma'am. And when he came to sell it to Mr Josh
ten years ago, I hear tell they had the almightiest row
anybody ever heard in this county. Seems your daddy
warn't happy about the terms and conditions of the sale.
Why some folks even say that——'

But what some folks said Penny never did find out,
for at that moment the door of the post office swung
open and Josh Miller strode in. The two women started
guiltily, and he flashed a sardonic look from one to the
other before he swept off the straw hat he was wearing.

'Talk of the devil!' muttered Betty Anne under her
breath.

'Good morning, Betty Anne,' murmured Josh silkily.
'Good morning, Miss Penny. Why, you two ladies look
real flushed. Are you having problems with your air-
conditioning, Betty Anne, or could it be you were talkin'
about me when I came in?'

Penny clenched her fists in annoyance. Why did Josh
Miller always have to put her at a disadvantage? Tossing
her head, she smiled coldly at him.

'Not at all, Mr Miller,' she replied sweetly. 'I was just
telling Mrs Summers about my plans for the future.'

'Yes, sir,' confirmed Betty Anne, gratefully clutching
at this lifeline. 'Why, Miss Penny tells me she's gonna
stay on here in Williamsburg County. She's already quit
her job and written to her mama about it!'

Betty Anne brandished Penny's letters as proof of what
she was saying. But Josh ignored her. Taking hold of
Penny's arm, he looked down into her hostile face.

'So you're really going to do it?' he demanded harshly.
'In spite of everything I've said to you, you're determined to stay on here?'

'Yes, I am,' said Penny through her teeth.

To her annoyance she found that her heart was
thudding unevenly. The touch of Josh's strong brown
fingers on her bare skin seemed to be sending unac-
countable flutters of sensation through her body and she
took a step backwards, hoping to shake off his grip. But

he was not so easy to dislodge. He flashed a swift glance at Betty Anne and his rugged features suddenly creased into a mocking smile.

'You know, it's real fortunate running into you like this, Miss Penny,' he purred. 'Seems like every time I come to see you at home, you're just too busy for callers. And I've got some neighbourly advice I want to give you about that land of yours. In fact, maybe you'd like to discuss it right now, while Betty Anne is here to add her two cents' worth. She knows more than anybody else about what goes on in this county.'

Penny fumed silently. No way was she going to have a quarrel with Josh under Betty Anne's interested gaze so that the whole affair could then be broadcast to all her neighbours! Much as she loathed Josh, she had to admit that his strategy was clever.

'No, I don't think so, Mr Miller,' she said bitterly. 'I think it would be better to discuss that in private.'

'Good,' murmured Josh in a silky voice. 'Then I'll be welcome if I drop by your house tonight?'

'Oh, Mr Miller,' simpered Penny, 'I'm sure you know how welcome you'll always be when you call to see me!'

Josh gave a low growl of laughter.

'Oh, I do, ma'am, I do,' he agreed. 'Shall we say after supper tonight, then?'

CHAPTER FOUR

FOR the life of her, Penny could not have explained the restlessness that took hold of her when she arrived back from the post office. She had planned to spend the afternoon painting, but instead she found herself vacuuming the house, polishing the pine dining-table, cutting fresh flowers to set in vases on every available surface. And, as if that weren't bad enough, she even dragged out the cookbook that Sarah McKendrick had given her and baked an enormous apple crumble. Once the house was filled with the rich, spicy scent of hot apple and cinnamon, she went into the tiny bathroom and drew a bath. Recklessly splashing in pine-scented foaming bath lotion, she looked at herself in the full-length mirror.

'Well, there's no reason why you shouldn't treat yourself once in a while,' she told her reflection defensively. 'And you haven't done any proper cooking for ages!'

But when she turned off the taps and lowered herself into the frothy, scented water, honesty overtook her.

'Who do you think you're kidding, Penelope Caroline Owen?' she demanded bitterly, as she reached for a flannel. 'You're doing all this for him, aren't you? Josh Miller himself!'

It baffled her that Josh should have such an unsettling effect on her. After all, she wasn't a naïve fifteen-year-old to go weak-kneed over a muscular brown body, a broad, hairy chest and a surly disposition. When she was much younger and extremely starry-eyed, she had always thought that violent physical attraction to a man would go hand in hand with falling passionately in love and then marrying him. Unfortunately life didn't seem

68

to work that way. The one man Penny had come close
to marrying had never reduced her to this fluttering state
of aching physical awareness. Simon had been stockily
built, slightly jowly and with a conversational repertoire
limited to corporate finance and the iniquities of the
Taxation Department. His lovemaking had been brisk,
predictable and vaguely unsatisfying. All in all, Penny
had found it rather a relief to be quit of it. But it was
certainly one of life's little ironies that she should now
find herself so devastatingly aroused by a man she didn't
even like. Every encounter she had with Josh Miller was
like a fast-moving sword fight in which she always came
off second best. Antagonism smouldered deep inside her
as she recalled the way he always bullied her and man-
ipulated her into doing whatever he wanted. Take this
meeting tonight, for instance. She hadn't wanted it, but
he had foisted it on her with his steely insistence on
having his own way. *I hate him, I hate him, I hate him!*
she thought rebelliously. *So why is it that whenever he
walks into a room, the air seems to crackle with electricity and I feel more vibrantly alive than I ever thought
possible?*

With an exasperated groan, she lay back in the water
and tried to banish Josh Miller's mocking green eyes
and sardonic smile from her mind. Pouring shampoo
into her cupped palm and then massaging it slowly into
her hair, she lectured herself sternly. *Don't be so stupid,
Penny. Just because he kissed you a couple of times it
doesn't mean that he wants a serious relationship with
you. And anyway, you can't stand the man, remember?*
All the same, she thought, ducking under the water and
rinsing her hair, *there's no harm in looking my best
tonight* ...

By nine-thirty that evening she did look her best. With
maddening vagueness, Josh had said only that he would
drop by after supper. It was hard to know what time
that meant, but Penny decided that it would be quite
reasonable for her to have a pot of coffee bubbling on

the stove and the apple crumble and cream still in a dish
on the dining-table. She could rise to her feet casually
and say, 'Oh, I was just eating my dessert. Maybe you'd
like to join me.' Then, when they'd sorted out the fact
that Penny wasn't going to be browbeaten into selling
her property, perhaps they'd actually get quite friendly.
Josh might enjoy the pie and they might sit on the sofa
together and discuss Penny's plans, and he might suddenly sweep her into his arms and kiss her... At this
point Penny's imagination came to a screeching halt and
she moved hastily across to the stove to put the coffee
on.

Thanks to Josh's intervention, the fan in the range
hood was now whisper-quiet and the whole room looked
cosy and inviting. The table was covered in a blue and
white checked cloth with a bunch of yellow and white
daisies in the centre. The apple crumble steamed invitingly in its dish and lamplight reflected softly off the
blue and white cups and the crystal port glasses. The
secondhand sofa was scattered invitingly with cushions
and all the magazines had been tidied off the coffee-
table. Penny had even kicked the department store cata-
logues out of sight under an armchair, and everything
was as ready as it would ever be for a guest. Restlessly
she tidied her hair in front of the mirror on the wall.
She hoped it didn't look too obvious that she had dressed
up to meet Josh—after all, the trim white blouse and
flared skirt with its pattern of luxuriant autumn-coloured
flowers was the sort of thing she might easily have worn
while on her own. And the brown eye-shadow, apricot-
coloured lipstick and hint of blusher on her cheeks were
very discreet. Even the pearl drop earrings in a gold
setting were the sort of thing any girl might just happen
to be wearing when somebody dropped in. Penny gave
her hair a final pat, then crossed the room. All her pre-
parations were complete and there was nothing more she
could do. Scooping a generous wedge of apple crumble

into a blue and white bowl, she sat down at the table to wait.

By ten o'clock the first pot of coffee had almost boiled dry and she had to throw it out and put another one on. By ten-thirty she had been back twice to the mirror to repair her make-up. And by eleven o'clock the warm, spicy apple crumble had gone cold and leaden in its dish. But it wasn't until midnight that Penny finally faced up to the truth.

'Damn Josh Miller!' she cried, jumping to her feet and slamming both her fists down on her carefully set table. 'He isn't coming at all. He's stood me up! If he ever shows his face around here again, I'm really going to send him packing!'

But Josh seemed in no hurry to show his face again. All week Penny fretted and fumed and longed for an opportunity to confront him, but apart from a single occasion when he waved to her from the back of a trail bike, she didn't even catch a glimpse of him. And on the two occasions when her doorbell rang, she was humiliated to see the eagerness with which she sprang to answer it, only to find that it wasn't Josh on the doorstep. Once it was Sarah McKendrick with a basket of vegetables and a slab of pound cake. And once it was the local minister calling to invite her to a church social. Penny was touched by their kindness, but she could not quell the aching sense of loneliness that invaded her after they left. The truth was that only one person would be able to banish that. And she knew perfectly well that he really didn't care about her.

All the same, when the phone rang the following Saturday evening, she rushed to answer it. She was just washing out her brushes in the kitchen sink while keeping a careless eye on her supper of baked beans when she heard its shrill tone. Grabbing a rag for her painty hands, she hastily picked up the receiver.

'Hello,' she said eagerly.

'Is that you, Miss Penny?'

Disappointment flooded her. It wasn't Josh, but some
woman.

'Yes,' replied Penny, puzzled.

'Wilma Cox speaking, honey. Remember me? I met
you at the Kingswood Hospital on your very first day
here.'

'Oh, yes, of course,' agreed Penny. 'How are you,
Mrs Cox? And how's Steve coming along after the
accident?'

'We're both just fine,' Mrs Cox assured her. 'But look,
honey, I've just called you with the rudest request you
can possibly imagine. Now you're free to say no, but
you sure would save my bacon if you'd say yes.'

'What is it?' asked Penny, intrigued.

'Well, it's this,' explained Wilma. 'I'm hosting the
Cotillion Ball for the local Daughters of the Confederacy
at my house tonight and, would you believe it, one of
the women has just called and told me she's stuck in
North Carolina with car trouble? Well, she ain't going
to make it to dinner, honey, and Mr Cox is cuttin' up
somethin' awful about it. Says we'll be the laughing stock
of the entire county if we sit down to dinner one short.
The way he's raisin' Cain about it, I figure there's goin'
to be more blood spilled than there was in the original
Civil War if I don't find somebody to take her place real
soon. Why, Mr Cox, he said to me, "Wilma, I don't
care if you invite the worst old hag in the County, just
so long as there's somebody a-sittin' in that chair come
eight o'clock tonight." Well, honey, naturally I thought
of you right away. And anyways, everybody else was
down at the beach or already out for the evening. So
can you help me out?'

Penny rocked with silent laughter at this unflattering
invitation, but as soon as she could speak, she answered
politely.

'I'd be glad to come, Mrs Cox,' she said sincerely.
'But from the sound of things this is a pretty formal

dinner, and I'm afraid I just don't have the clothes to cope with something like that.'

'Oh, honey, that's no problem,' Mrs Cox assured her. 'My daughter Laney is home from college on her summer vacation. She's just about your build, and she's got a closet full of evening dresses she could lend you. So how about if I send her over to get you right away?'

'OK,' agreed Penny recklessly, switching off the baked beans. 'I'll be ready and waiting for her.'

Laney proved to be a lanky brunette with a contagious grin and a ready flow of conversation. In spite of being taller than Penny, she was much the same shape and only too willing to lend her clothes in a good cause. She was also a mine of information about everybody in Williamsburg County, and by the time they reached the Coxes' plantation Penny's head was spinning with details about the other guests who were expected. As they sped up the gravel driveway under a canopy of live oaks, Penny was struck by the resemblance to Waterford Hall. Although the house was a shade smaller than Josh's home, it had the same kind of formal grounds and white columns at the front entrance. Laney hustled her through the entrance hall, where a distracted Mrs Cox paused to greet her before launching into a lament about burnt sweet potatoes, then piloted her expertly up the curving staircase to her bedroom.

'Don't let Mama bother you,' she advised, kicking off her shoes and stretching out on the bed. 'She enjoys creating a fuss like that. The dinner will be OK.'

'Are you coming?' asked Penny, warming to the vivacious brunette.

Laney grinned.

'Are you kidding?' she retorted. 'I'm going out for pizza with my boyfriend. So you just take a look in my closet and choose anything you like. Except my Air Jordan track shoes—I don't lend those to nobody. Anyways, you couldn't wear them to a cotillion ball. We're talking formal tonight.'

'How formal?' asked Penny with a sinking feeling, as she opened the closet.

Laney stretched and yawned.

'Early nineteenth century,' she said. 'The guys will all be wearing white ties and tails, so I guess you'd better go for one of those crinoline dresses near the end. But I'm warning you, they're murder when you need to go to the bathroom.'

Penny's eyes widened as she chose a dusky gold dress with multi-tiered, billowing skirts and no visible means of support.

'Where's the bodice?' she asked.

Laney giggled.

'Search me,' she replied. 'I guess they figured if you've got it, flaunt it. That hem's a mite long for you, so just mind you don't step on it when you're dancing, 'cause you're liable to lose the entire dress.'

Penny shuddered.

'What else do I need to know?' she asked.

'Not much,' shrugged Laney. 'They'll have a waiter calling out the names when you go into dinner and you take your partner's arm and go into the dining-room with him. And when the ball starts, you'll have a programme for the dances where you write down your partner's name. Etiquette says you have to dance at least once with anyone who asks you. After about midnight, it's not so formal. They usually have a scavenger hunt, and people wind up necking on the bridge of the duckpond and that kind of thing.'

'You're joking!' exclaimed Penny in disbelief.

Laney giggled again.

'It's a gas,' she assured her. 'You'll enjoy yourself. Just make sure you wind up with somebody good-looking for the scavenger hunt.'

Not in the least reassured by Laney's advice, Penny made her way nervously down the stairs half an hour later. The huge gilt mirror on the landing reassured her that she looked her best. Laney had wound her heavy

corn-coloured hair into a coronet on top of her head and
fastened a heavy necklace of gold and topaz around her
throat. But she felt as if she had an embarrassingly large
amount of naked brown flesh exposed above the low-
cut neckline of the frock. And her voluminous crinoline
required a lot of caution if she were not to knock over
any of the silver-framed photos or delicate pieces of china
that filled the house. Taking a deep breath, Penny glided
sedately down the staircase with one slim hand resting
on the railing.

'Well, what a pleasant surprise!' said a husky masculine voice, as she alighted at the foot of the stairs.

'Josh Miller!' hissed Penny, momentarily disconcerted.

'At your service, ma'am,' he replied, lifting her hand
to his lips in a parody of the nineteenth-century
gentleman. 'Is there anything I can get for you? A glass
of champagne, perhaps? Or one of those shrimp cocktails on sticks? Or would you like me to step outside the
front door so that you can have the pleasure of slamming
it in my face in full view of half the County?'

For a moment Penny was so furious that she actually
contemplated doing exactly that, but then sanity pre-
vailed. The entrance hall was already filling up and there
was a steady hum of conversation. To snub Josh now
would be social suicide. If she were going to go on living
with these people, she would have to be polite to him at
least on the surface. Smiling graciously, she fluttered her
eyelashes at him.

'You set this up, didn't you?' she demanded in a
furious undertone.

Josh smiled modestly.

'Let's just say that I used my influence,' he conceded
smugly.

'It seems like a lot of trouble to go to for very little
result,' said Penny through her teeth.

'Oh, I wouldn't say that it was for very little result,'
replied Josh, smiling charmingly at an elderly dowager
who was gliding past. 'I wanted to talk to you, Penny.'

'Then you could have come to see me last Monday, the way you promised,' she retorted.

Josh's smile set into a dangerous line.

'Ah, but that encounter would have been entirely on your terms,' he murmured regretfully. 'And I like to feel in control of a situation.'

'Really?' asked Penny. 'How nice. But where I come from, it's considered rather rude to invite yourself to somebody's house and then not show up.'

'Is it?' he replied blandly. 'How interesting. Now where I come from, it's considered mighty rude to slam the door in somebody's face, invited or not.'

Penny flinched, and Josh pressed home his advantage. Moving closer so that the threatening bulk of his body shielded her from the other guests, he looked down at her with glittering green eyes.

'You've been making a fool out of me for the past month, Miss Penny,' he said softly. 'And I thought it was time you had a taste of your own medicine, so when my partner cancelled tonight, I asked Wilma to call you up and invite you. And here you are eating out of my hand. Now I call that mighty satisfactory.'

'I am not eating out of your hand,' protested Penny in a furious stage whisper.

'Oh, no?' he queried mildly. 'Then just watch this, sweetheart. And keep in mind that the way you behave in the next couple of hours will determine how you're received in this County for the rest of your life. Mrs McClary! I wonder if you'd be so good as to step over here a moment, ma'am. There's a young lady I'd like to present to you.'

Penny watched in silent rage as an elderly woman with a complexion like mahogany barged through the crowd and scrutinised her through a set of powerful bifocals.

'I'd like you to meet a friend of mine, Miss Penny Owen from Sydney, Australia,' murmured Josh smoothly.

He gave Penny a swift pinch on the arm, so that she jumped and then extended her hand.

'How do you do?' she gabbled.

Josh smiled benignly and continued as if there had been no interruption.

'Penny, this is Mildred Inglesby McClary. Her ancestors came over to America on the *Mayflower*.'

'Australia!' exclaimed the old woman. 'My land, whatever next? Still, any friend of yours is a friend of the McClarys, Josh. Glad to meet you, Miss Penny. Now, I'm having a covered dish supper for our local church at my house next Saturday at seven-thirty and we surely would like to see you there. You cain't miss us, honey, we're the last house on the left just outside of Clarksville. Be sure and come, now!'

'Thank you very much,' replied Penny in a sinking voice.

'See?' murmured Josh maliciously, as Mildred McClary disappeared back into the milling throng.

'So what does that prove?' demanded Penny hotly.

'It proves that you are in my power and that you'll do exactly as I say tonight,' he replied in a steely voice. 'Won't you, sugar?'

'No,' seethed Penny. 'I hate you, Josh Miller! I'm fed up to the back teeth with your bullying, and you needn't think I'll do a damned thing you tell me, because I won't! So there!'

'Is that right?' purred Josh.

His fingers rested for a moment on the nape of her neck and he fluttered them gently. The motion sent an exquisitely erotic thrill through Penny's body, but there was a hint of menace in it too. She wondered what he would do if she simply turned and walked out of the house right this minute. Would he put up with the embarrassment of letting her go, or would he endure the even greater embarrassment of fetching her back? She looked up and saw him watching her with an amused, provocative expression in his narrowed green eyes.

'Just try it,' he whispered.

Penny's cheeks stained with colour.

'I don't know what you're talking about,' she retorted.

'Good,' drawled Josh. 'Then come and meet the rest of the County before we're called in to dinner.'

Half an hour later they were summoned into the magnificent dining-room. Of course, it was too much to hope that she would be seated anywhere other than beside Josh, but Penny found that her companion on the other side was a pleasant young attorney. He introduced himself as Harvey Anderson and was soon deep in conversation with her about a planned vacation to Australia. To Penny's relief Josh seemed content to devote himself to the woman on his other side, and after a few minutes she began to relax. For the first time she was able to notice the gleaming chandeliers, the lovingly polished silver, the delicate china and the colourful costumes.

As the meal progressed, there was a constant low hum of conversation and laughter all about her, and she wished for a moment that she could have come in different circumstances. The food was excellent. South Carolina crab soup, hot, thick and warming, was followed by an entrée of oysters and a dazzling array of main courses and side dishes. Harvey was anxious for her to try all the local specialities, and she soon found her plate loaded with roast turkey, candied yams, red rice, asparagus casserole and the tasty barbecued pork that was Williamsburg County's favourite dish. But she might as well have been eating barbecued sandpaper for all the impression it made on her. For she had discovered that eating dinner next to Josh Miller was rather like sitting down to a meal on the San Andreas fault when all the seismographs were registering nine on the Richter scale. Staring at his fierce profile with the powerful neck emerging from the snowy shirt and the sleek dark hair gleaming above his collar, she had a horrified realisation that she wanted to reach out and touch him.

'So do they have any commercial use at all?' asked Harvey.

Penny dragged her wandering concentration back and tried desperately to remember what they had been discussing. The Barrier Reef. Marine species. Sharks?

'Oh, yes,' she said enthusiastically. 'We eat them. I just love them fried in batter.'

Harvey looked horrified.

'Crown of thorns starfish?' he echoed incredulously.

Penny winced.

'I'm sorry,' she apologised contritely, 'I'm afraid I lost the thread for a moment. But tell me, Mr Anderson, you mentioned before that your hobby was genealogy. Do you know anything about the Eliot family, by any chance? My father——'

'Harvey, was that you who handled that spray-painting prosecution over in Andrews last fall?' cut in Josh. 'Because if so, I want to tell you that you did a mighty fine job with it. Why, I believe that guy was wanted in three states for stealing cars and repainting them.'

Penny was left fuming as Harvey shrugged modestly and assured Josh that it 'warn't nothing'. And she never had a chance to return to the subject of her father, for the waiters soon returned to take away the empty dishes and set out the desserts. By the time Josh had helped her charmingly to pecan pie with whipped cream, Harvey had turned with relief to the woman on his other side.

'Why did you interrupt us like that?' hissed Penny, as Josh passed the cream further down the table.

'Honey, that guy is so boring when he gets on the subject of genealogy, I figured I was doing a public service. Anyway, he's quite happy now, making eyes at Vicky Anne Walker there.'

'Sure,' agreed Penny sourly. 'She probably doesn't eat crown of thorns starfish.'

'What?'

'Oh, never mind. When does this dinner end anyway?'

It didn't end until nearly eleven o'clock. In spite of the warm hospitality, the delicious food and the beautiful surroundings, Penny was so strung up with tension that she could not enjoy herself. Throughout the meal she was conscious of the cruel, sardonic glitter in Josh Miller's eyes each time he glanced at her. Oh, he might turn on that easygoing Southern charm for everybody else, but when it came to dealing with Penny the charm was replaced by a ruthless determination to humiliate her. The thought of having her so blatantly under his control clearly acted as a kind of aphrodisiac to him. More than once through the course of the dinner he glanced lazily at her with an expression that made her feel like a slave girl put up for auction. And the angry flash of her eyes in response obviously filled him with triumphant amusement.

She grew more panicky with each passing minute as she remembered Laney's uncensored comments about the scavenger hunt. Hadn't she said something about people kissing in the gardens? Would Josh really inflict that on her as the final humiliation? Obviously he was still smarting over the way she had shut him out of her house, but surely he wouldn't take that sort of revenge? Would he? Penny stole an apprehensive glance at him and found herself saluted with an upraised champagne glass, narrowed green eyes and a crooked smile. Oh, yes, he would, she thought, with a sinking sensation. Hysteria took hold of her and she caught her breath. Whatever happened, she vowed, she would not let Josh Miller be her partner for the scavenger hunt. Yet when it came to it, she actually had no choice.

As a way of inducing her guests to circulate, Wilma Cox had been visited by the happy inspiration of giving everybody an envelope containing half the title of a nursery rhyme. The guests then had to mingle in the ballroom, chanting their phrase until they met their other half. Feeling intensely foolish, Penny trailed around the floor bleating 'Baa, Baa!' and she was certain it was the hand of malevolent fate which sent Josh strolling across to claim her.

'Hi,' he said, giving her a slow, insulting smile. 'I guess you realise I'm the Black Sheep.'

Penny's eyes darkened with panic.

'I think I'd rather sit this one out,' she said faintly.

'I don't doubt it,' he growled, laying one steely hand under her arm and propelling her ruthlessly towards the door. 'But I don't recall giving you my permission to do that, ma'am.'

She fired up at that.

'Your permission?' she demanded in a furious undertone. 'I don't need your permission to do anything, Mr Miller!'

Josh smiled grimly.

'Oh, yes, you do, Miss Penny,' he replied huskily. 'You're only at this ball because I arranged it. And if you want any kind of social life in this County from today onwards, you're going to have to keep my goodwill. So you're going to do exactly as I say, honey, whether you like it or not. And yes, that does include being kissed in the shrubbery, if that's what I choose to demand. Got it?'

'You brute!' snapped Penny.

She took a couple of swift, uneven breaths as they made their way across the patio and down the steps to the lawn. Holding herself rigidly erect, she tried to pull away from Josh's grip, but with a low growl of laughter, he dragged her against him and his fingers pressed more firmly into her arm. She could not help being acutely conscious of his powerful, virile body so close beside her and the warm, sensual heaviness of the night that seemed like an invitation to love. Her skirts made a soft, rustling sound like the lapping of waves as she walked, and there was a full moon highlighting the shapes of the live oak trees with their trailing garlands of Spanish moss. The air was soft and still and teeming with the rustle of katydids and night-flying birds. As they passed the side

porch of the house, there was a muffled giggle and a
blurred shape separated out into two figures, a tall man
in a dark suit and tails and a girl in a crinoline dress.
Penny turned her gaze hastily away and marched determinedly on, feeling agonisingly aware of Josh's warm
fingers clasping her formally under the arm. As they
crossed the sweeping lawn near the back of the house
and came to a halt on the bridge near the duckpond,
she pulled her arm irritably out of his grasp.

'Do you think we can stop the Victorian formalities
now?' she demanded.

'Why?' asked Josh with a shrug. 'I kind of enjoy
holding you.'

She could hear the amusement in his voice and it made
her angrier than ever.

'This is so stupid!' she stormed. 'Pretending we're
back in the eighteen-forties and all that Baa! Baa! stuff.
Why did Mrs Cox have to pair me off with you anyway?'

'Don't blame her,' shrugged Josh. 'She always pairs
off lovers.'

'We're not lovers!' retorted Penny.

'Maybe we should be,' he murmured throatily, and
without warning he drew his hand down her bosom and
brought it to a halt just inside her low-cut bodice. 'What
do you say?'

For a moment she could say nothing at all. Her heart
seemed to be beating a frantic tattoo under the warm
pressure of Josh's fingers and her breath remained stuck
in her throat. But if she had lost the power of speech,
she soon regained the power of action. Raising her hand,
she gave an angry sob and slapped him hard across the
face. He reeled and touched his cheek.

'Is that yes or no?' he asked.

Penny let out her breath in a furious gasp.

'Can't you take no for an answer about anything?'
she demanded despairingly.

He gave a mirthless laugh and drew her into his arms.

'Not about you, that's for damned sure,' he said. 'I want you, Penny. I want you so bad it's just burning me up. I've been lying awake every night for the last month thinking about you, worrying about how you were getting on in that little gimcracky trailer, wishing I could get to see you somehow...'

Penny found that her hair had slipped out of its coils and was being wound around his fingers. She also found that his face was buried against her throat and that the rough after-five stubble on his cheek was sending prickles of excitement through her entire body as he kissed her slender neck. Once. And then again. Her senses reeled with the hateful, familiar discovery that however much she detested him, he still had the power to excite her unbearably. She gave a low whimper of longing and her hands clenched convulsively as she tried to push him away.

'Oh, Josh, please!' she gasped. 'Don't do it to me! I know you're only trying to humiliate me, and I can't stand it!'

Her dark eyes gleamed in the moonlight as she stared imploringly up at him, but her plea was wasted. His features twisted into an angry, relentless mask and his hands tightened on her arms.

'Is that what you think?' he demanded hoarsely.

'Why not? It's the truth, isn't it?'

'Part of it. But there's more to it than that.'

'What do you mean?' cried Penny.

'Just that there's something about you that drives me crazy, honey. And I know it's the same for you. Maybe you think you hate my guts, but you're wrong. There's something really powerful between us, Penny, really special. And it sure isn't hate.'

Penny caught her breath and stood gazing uncertainly at him. Her head whirled and she felt as if Josh had swung her right off balance. Was he trying to tell her that he really cared for her? The thought was so strange, so unsettling that she raised one hand defensively as if to ward off the panic that overtook her.

'Are you fixing to take another swing at me?' he asked seriously.

Penny flinched guiltily.

'Oh, Josh!' she muttered, her fingers travelling uncertainly up to touch his cheek. 'I didn't hurt you before, did I?'

'It's agony,' he replied. 'Pure agony. Of course, it might help if you kissed it better.'

She hesitated, feeling bewildered. Then with a sudden, exasperated giggle, she rose on tiptoe and pecked him lightly on the cheek. His mouth immediately moved down and claimed hers in a warm, lingering kiss. For thirty satisfying seconds Penny gave herself up to the blissful sensations that were coursing through her. The skilful caress of Josh's hands moving in wavelike rhythms across her shoulders and back, the deep, pulsating excitement that was flaring through her, the agonisingly sensual touch of his lips on hers. Then she broke slowly away and came back down to earth.

'Oh, Josh,' she complained with a long sigh. 'You are totally unscrupulous!'

'Totally,' he agreed, pressing a kiss into the palm of her hand and closing her fingers over it. 'But I've missed you so bad, Penny, I'd have done anything to get to see you again.'

Penny's lips curved into a doubtful smile. It was hard to believe that the swashbuckling Josh Miller could really be whispering such tender words to her.

'Truly?' she asked with a quiver in her voice.

'Truly,' he agreed, nuzzling the top of her tumbled hair. 'You're some girl, Penny Owen. I've never met anybody quite like you.'

For fully ten seconds Penny stood breathlessly gazing up into his intent face. What she saw there made her wonder whether she really hated him so much after all.

And suddenly her hostility slipped away, to be replaced by a hesitant new tenderness.

'And you're some guy, Josh Miller,' she murmured uncertainly. 'I've never met anybody quite like you either.'

'Well, ain't that touching?' demanded a crystalline voice behind them. 'I declare, I never heard anything quite so sweet!'

Penny swung round in horror to see a glamorous dark-haired woman in a red crinoline holding a lamp above her head. The other woman's face looked as perfect and expressionless as a lingerie mannequin's, except for her eyes. They were indigo blue and blazing with malice as she glared at her. Instinctively Penny shrank back, and felt Josh's arm tighten protectively around her. Josh didn't seem in the least disturbed by this strange encounter. In fact, he seemed to relish it.

'Well, hi there,' he said in a voice vibrant with amusement. 'Good to see you again, Brenda Sue.'

CHAPTER FIVE

FOR a moment they all remained motionless, like cricketers frozen for an action replay. Then Josh came to life.

'Penny, this is Brenda Sue Hartley,' he said. 'Brenda Sue, I'd like you to meet Penny Owen.'

'No, thanks,' sneered Brenda Sue. 'I don't mix with poor white trash.'

Penny caught her breath indignantly, but before she could say a word, Josh retaliated.

'Really?' he murmured pleasantly. 'Then what were you doing spending a night in the mountains with Greg Alden?'

It was Brenda Sue's turn to catch her breath.

'Who told you about Greg?' she demanded hoarsely.

Josh's face was set in harsh lines in the flickering glow from the lantern.

'My cousin Mary Ellen Manning,' he replied evenly. 'She was staying in the same hotel and she saw you come down to breakfast together.'

'Why couldn't she mind her own goddamned business?' seethed Brenda Sue.

'Well, she kinda thought it was her business to let me know,' explained Josh with a touch of regret. 'You know, I really don't like being two-timed, Brenda Sue. Especially with some two-bit entrepreneur like Greg Alden.'

'So you thought you'd have your revenge, did you, honey?' crooned Brenda Sue, letting her eyes wander insultingly over Penny's figure. 'Well, I sure would have thought you could have done better for yourself than that!'

Penny stood speechless for a moment as a raging groundswell of indignation and embarrassment swept through her. To think she had been fool enough to be-

lieve the things Josh Miller had said to her tonight, to
believe that he really did think she was special and feel
attracted to her for her own sake! Whereas all the time
he had only been out for revenge on his thoroughly un-
pleasant girlfriend. Well, damn both of them! Penny regained her voice.

'Well, I can see you two lovebirds are longing to be
back in each other's arms after this trivial misunder-
standing,' she announced in a low, angry voice. 'So
please don't let me stand in your way, because I really
feel that you charming people deserve each other. Now,
if you'll excuse me, I'm leaving.'

She paused for a moment, as if struck by a sudden
thought, then turned and slapped Josh smartly on his
other cheek. After that, she gathered up her skirts and
fled like a deer across the wide green lawn.

'Penny!' thundered Josh. 'Come back here, damn it!'

But Penny had the advantage of surprise and Brenda
Sue was clinging to Josh's arm, her voice raised in a
furious tirade. With a single backward glance at the figures struggling in the lamplight, Penny sprinted towards the gravel driveway that looped past the front
door—and almost went straight under the wheels of an
arriving car.

'Holy Toledo!' cried a girl, looking out of the driver's
side window. 'Is that you, Penny?'

'Laney!' cried Penny. 'Oh, thank goodness! Look,
please, please don't ask any questions. Just drive me
home, would you?'

They were halfway back to Merivale before Laney
could get anything more than breathless gasping and
muffled vows of revenge out of Penny.

'Look, honey,' cried Laney for the fourth time, 'I
don't want to be nosy or nothing, I just want to hear
every delicious, squalid detail. What exactly did Josh
Miller do to you? And why were he and Brenda Sue
Hartley wrestling near the duckpond? C'mon, spill the
beans!'

'I hate him!' wailed Penny. 'The swine! I just couldn't bear to spend another minute with him.'

'Oh, yeah? Well, you're gonna have to do a bit better than that, honey! I'll have to cook up some kind of story to tell my mama about why you left the way you did.'

Penny stopped in mid-wail, utterly appalled.

'Your mother!' she echoed. 'Oh, Laney, I forgot all about your mother! What on earth am I going to say to her?'

Laney relented.

'Aw, don't worry,' she said reassuringly. 'I'll tell her you wrenched your ankle down by the duckpond and I had to take you back to Kingswood for another X-ray. How's that?'

Penny winced.

'All right,' she agreed despairingly. 'You're a pal, Laney.'

'No sweat,' replied Laney cheerfully. 'Now come on, honey. The truth!'

'I can't,' protested Penny. 'It's too sordid!'

'Great!' enthused Laney.

In the end she did drag every last embarrassing detail out of Penny. By then they were sitting in Penny's tiny kitchen over their second cup of coffee and Laney had her long legs draped over one of the chairs. She was gratifying indignant about Josh's behaviour.

'Gee, men are such skunks!' she complained. 'But what are you gonna do now, Penny?'

'Do?' echoed Penny.

'Yeah. I mean, from everything you've told me about Josh, he's gonna be round here pounding on the door come nine o'clock in the morning, demanding to possess your house or your body or both! So what are you doing to do?'

Penny flinched.

'I see what you mean!' she said miserably.

Laney rocked thoughtfully back in her chair, till it hung precariously on two legs.

'I'll tell you what,' she suggested. 'Come down to the
beach with me. We've got a place at Myrtle Beach and
I've been fixing to go down there anyway for a break.
Nobody but me will know you're there and Josh won't
be able to trace you.'

'Won't your mother tell him I'm there?' objected
Penny.

'Mama? No, she don't hardly go near the place.
Anyways, she's still too busy nursing Steve to leave home.
And you can send a card to her saying you met some
Australian friends and went off with them for a vacation
to get over your new sprained ankle. A card without an
address, of course.'

Penny gazed at her in awe.

'Laney, you have a criminal mind,' she said
admiringly.

Laney grinned.

'I know,' she sighed. 'Terrible, ain't it? And me
studying Business Administration too! So you'll do it,
then?'

Penny took a long, uneven breath.

'I'll do it!' she agreed.

The Coxes' beach house was unlike any holiday home
that Penny had ever visited before. She had gone to
Myrtle Beach expecting a modest bungalow with wooden
bunks, a single gas ring and an outside lavatory, but instead she found a lavishly appointed miniature mansion.
There were five bedrooms, three bathrooms, an
enormous living-room and kitchen, along with an assortment of sun-decks and screened porches. The whole
place looked like a set of illustrations from *Better Homes
and Gardens*, and it soon became apparent that Laney
expected a lifestyle to match. For the first couple of days,
the two girls went on a whirlwind of shopping in the
nearby malls, played mini golf or went to amusement
parks and dined out in the evening. But on the third day,
Penny decided she would have to call a halt to this ex-

travagance. As Laney flung herself down on the chintz-
covered couch in a housecoat and began buffing her
nails, Penny steeled herself for the necessary
explanations.

'So where do you want to eat tonight?' asked Laney.
'There's a real nice seafood place that just opened up at
Murrells Inlet that we could try if you want.'

'I'm sorry, Laney,' said Penny bluntly. 'I just can't
afford to eat out every night.'

Laney looked horrified.

'Oh, honey, why didn't you say?' she demanded. 'Gee,
I should have thought of that. But listen, don't let it
worry you. I'll be glad to treat you.'

'No, Laney, really. There's no way I can return the
favour, so I just can't accept. But thank you anyway,
and please don't let me stop you from going if you want
to.'

Laney took a good deal of persuading, but in the end
she agreed to phone some other friends, and before long
she departed in an uproarious convoy bound for Murrells
Inlet. Left alone, Penny flung herself down on the exquisite floral sofa and let out a despairing sigh. It was
the first quiet moment she had had since the disastrous
night of the Cotillion Ball, but her thoughts were in
turmoil.

'Oh, help, I've made such a hash of things,' she
groaned. 'And it's all Josh Miller's fault.'

Try as she would, she could not banish his image from
her mind. Even during her sleep, she had vague, turbulent dreams of being swept into his arms and kissed
violently. And somehow, during her dreams, she did not
react with the outrage that her conscious mind would
have felt. Instead she always kissed him back with a
passion to equal his own. And then woke with an unbearable sense of loneliness and loss. The humiliating
fact was that she wanted Josh Miller, wanted him with
an urgency that sent a hot, throbbing pulse of desire
through her entire body whenever she thought about him.

It was not as if she loved him, she hastened to reassure herself. After all, his behaviour with Brenda Sue proved beyond doubt that he was a heartless, two-timing, vindictive swine. It was just that he had a certain coarse animal magnetism that made women go weak at the knees when they looked at him. Even sensible women like Penny Owen.

'I've just got to put enough distance between myself and him,' said Penny aloud. 'Coming down here was a good idea, but I'll have to do better than that. Perhaps I could go on a sketching trip up to the mountains or something like that. But I'll need more money for that. Maybe I could get a job...'

As always, having a project acted like a tonic for Penny. Next morning, she went out whistling for her early morning swim and then returned with the news that she was going job-hunting. A yawning Laney waved her off and was still in her pyjamas on the back porch when Penny returned at lunchtime.

'Guess what?' carolled Penny. 'I got a job as a waitress in a pizza parlour, starting today. Just on a trial basis for the rest of the week.'

Laney flinched.

'Oh, honey!' she exclaimed. 'You're gonna just hate that. You wait and see.'

But Laney's gloomy prediction proved false. For the first four days Penny had a wonderful time. In the mornings she swam and painted on the beach, in the afternoons she gossiped with Laney and in the evenings she whizzed around at the speed of light with trayloads of pizzas and spaghetti and submarine sandwiches. Until Saturday afternoon, when everything went totally and horribly wrong.

She had been asked to do the lunchtime shift, and by four o'clock she was glad to see that the crowds were finally thinning out. Her feet ached, there was a splash of tomato purée on her frilly white apron and her blonde hair was escaping from under her candy-striped cap. But

Antonio, the proprietor, seemed pleased with her as he ran his cutting wheel expertly through a sizzling pizza.

'You did real good for your first week,' he said, stowing the pizza in a box and ringing up the sale. 'And fifty cents is your change. Thank you, sir. So do you want to come back next week, Penny?'

'Yes, please,' agreed Penny.

'OK, well, do that. And I guess you can leave for today. No, hold it. Serve that couple who just came in first, would ya?'

'Sure,' said Penny, picking up a pair of menus and turning around.

But her smile froze on her face. For the couple who had just walked in were none other than Josh Miller and Brenda Sue Hartley. With a low gasp of dismay, Penny shrank back behind the cappuccino machine and tried to look invisible. Antonio gave her a strange look.

'Would you quit actin' so weird and get out and serve those people?' he asked curtly.

Reluctantly Penny picked up the menus and inched her way out on to the restaurant floor. Josh and Brenda Sue had already taken their places in an intimate booth in one corner of the restaurant. As she drew closer, Penny noticed that Brenda Sue had one perfectly manicured hand laid possessively on Josh's hairy brown arm. She was talking in a passionate undertone, but she broke off as Penny drew near—and then did a double-take as she recognised her.

'Well, well, well,' she said in a voice dripping with malice, 'if it ain't Little Orphan Annie herself! You know, Josh, I think we ought to go eat someplace else. They don't seem real particular about the kind of people they employ here.'

She half rose out of her seat, but Josh's powerful brown hand closed around her wrist.

'Sit down, Brenda Sue,' he growled.

There was a moment's tense silence and Penny felt his eyes raking fiercely over her body. She blushed under their searing scrutiny.

'I've been looking for you,' murmured Josh softly.

Penny caught Antonio's exasperated look and thrust the menus desperately on to the table.

'Perhaps you'd like to think for a while before you order,' she muttered, glancing around for an escape route.

'Well, maybe you can suggest something,' purred Brenda Sue. 'You must know a lot about junk food, working in a place like this.'

Penny flinched, but held her temper in check.

'The spaghetti bolognese is very good,' she suggested.

Brenda Sue's gaze alighted on the splash of sauce on Penny's apron.

'Provided you're not a messy eater,' she agreed.

'Or then again you could try the submarine sandwiches,' retorted Penny sweetly. 'They come in large or small, but we only recommend the large ones for people with unusually big mouths.'

Brenda Sue's exquisite face flushed dark with annoyance and Josh was seized by a sudden coughing fit. With an expression of consternation on his face, Antonio left the cash register and began to cross the floor.

'Your waitress insulted me!' stormed Brenda Sue as he approached them. 'I won't stay in this place a moment longer! Come on, Josh, let's go and eat at Murrells Inlet.'

'I've got a better idea,' replied Josh in his lazy drawl. 'You go eat at Murrells Inlet, Brenda Sue. I've got things I want to discuss with Penny.'

Brenda Sue gave a snort of outrage.

'I'll tell you what I think of your precious Penny——' she began, but Josh cut in.

'Don't,' he said in a deadly cold voice. 'You'll regret it if you do, Brenda Sue.'

'Damn you, Josh Miller!' hissed Brenda Sue. 'And damn you too, Miss Goody Two-Shoes!'

With another indignant snort, she stormed out of the restaurant, slamming the door behind her.

'OK, Penny, let's go,' urged Josh, rising to his feet.

'But, hey, what about your dinner, sir?' demanded the horrified Antonio, brandishing the menus.

Josh paused thoughtfully.

'I'll take two Pizza Napoletanas to go,' he said. 'And the waitress.'

Antonio blinked.

'Excuse me, sir?' he murmured in a failing voice.

Josh's perfect white teeth flashed in a sudden grin.

'I said I'll take the waitress too,' he explained, gripping Penny's arm. 'She's caused me so much trouble that I'm not letting her go now I've found her.'

'Caused you trouble?' echoed Antonio. 'How about the trouble she's caused me? I've bin runnin' this place three years now and I've never had a scene like that before!'

He turned to Penny.

'You're fired!' he said. 'As of tomorrow.'

Penny opened her mouth to protest, but Josh beat her to it.

'No, she isn't,' he retorted. 'She's quitting. As of right now. Get your bag, Penny.'

Penny was too shocked to argue, but as they walked out into the car park ten minutes later she heaved an exasperated sigh.

'You've got a nerve!' she complained. 'I needed that job, and now, thanks to you and Brenda Sue, I've been thrown out.'

Josh chuckled unrepentantly, as he stowed the pizzas in the back of the car. Then he unlocked the passenger door and held it open.

'I wouldn't worry about it if I were you,' he said carelessly. 'I don't think you belong in a pizza parlour. Now will you just quit complaining and get in the car?'

'No, I won't!' retorted Penny. 'Why should I?'

'Because I love you, you stupid girl!' exclaimed Josh fiercely. 'Now get in, will you?'

Penny's senses reeled.

'What did you say?' she whispered.

'I said you're a stupid girl,' replied Josh wearily.

'No, before that,' she insisted, swallowing hard.

His face lit up in one of his rare smiles. His hands descended, pinioning her against the car. Then he took a deep, slow breath like a man starved for oxygen who suddenly emerges out of water into the air.

'Oh, I've missed you,' he murmured softly. 'Do you know how much I've missed you, Penny?'

She shook her head wonderingly.

'I've been searching for you ever since that damned party,' he said, rubbing one hand wearily over his forehead. 'Look, why don't you come back to my place and we'll talk about it?'

'Your place?' she echoed, startled. 'You mean Waterford Hall?'

Josh shook his head.

'No,' he replied. 'I have a beach house about ten miles from here at Pawleys Island. I had a hunch you were in this area, so I came down to stay while I looked for you. Come and have a pizza with me and I'll tell you all about it.'

'All right,' she agreed half shyly.

She seemed incapable of saying anything except the most foolish, obvious things, but perhaps that was because the world had just shifted magically on its axis. Josh's curt admission that he loved her had brought everything into place like a new and wonderful pattern in a kaleidoscope. For weeks now she had been aching with resentment, believing that she hated him. Now she realised how wrong she had been. If she hadn't been head over heels in love with him from the very first moment, his antagonism would never have infuriated her so much. She gave a low gurgle of laughter at the realisation.

'What is it?' he asked, lifting one eyebrow.

'I just realised that you're only able to drive me insane because I'm so much in love with you.'

Josh's hand reached out and gripped hers hard.

'I'm ahead of you, honey,' he said hoarsely. 'I realised the exact same thing about you the night of the ball.'

They exchanged smiles that were tense with unspoken longing. Penny looked out at the shops that were flashing by, half concealed in the leafy greenery of the forests. Her head was spinning with Josh's revelation and she tried hard to work out what she really wanted from their relationship. But it all seemed to be remarkably simple. What she wanted was to be in his arms and in his bed, wearing his ring on her finger, carrying his children in her body and going through life beside him. She flashed him another hesitant smile, and he met it with a look that made her bones turn to water.

'One of these days very soon, I'm going to strip you totally naked and kiss every inch of your body,' he said in a smouldering voice. 'So how about that, Miss Penny?'

'Please,' agreed Penny fervently.

He gave a low growl of laughter.

'You're downright shameless, Miss Penny,' he murmured appreciatively.

Before long they turned off on the side road leading to Pawleys Island and the trees gave way to marshlands. Ribbons of pale blue water meandered slowly through golden reedbeds and children with rolled-up jeans and crabbing nets waved to them from the muddy shallows. A white egret glided lazily down over the car and settled on the end of a wooden jetty before smoothly folding its wings. The scene was lit with a soft golden light from the late afternoon sun, but ominous grey clouds were massing overhead.

'Looks like a storm brewing,' said Josh, gazing keenly out of the window. 'Well, at least we'll be inside by the time it breaks.'

He was right. In less than five minutes the car came
to a halt underneath a tall yellow house built on stilts
overlooking the ocean. As they climbed out, a sudden
gust of wind whipped Penny's skirt around her legs and
stinging particles of sand made them both screw up their
eyes. The heat was so overpowering that it was like being
in a hothouse.

'I hope Laney's all right,' she shouted above the wind.
'She's gone out mackerel fishing with some of her
friends.'

'She should be fine,' Josh reassured her. 'Any skipper
in his right mind would turn and head for shelter at the
first sign of bad weather. Now you go on up and I'll
bring the pizzas.'

A moment later Penny was in the front hall of Josh's
house, blinking the sand out of her eyes and surveying
herself ruefully in the gilt mirror on the wall. Josh
stepped past her into the kitchen and deposited the pizzas
in the oven, while she was still examining her bedraggled
hair and stained uniform.

'I look awful,' she complained.

He emerged from the kitchen and stood behind her
with his hands on her shoulders. She saw his warm,
teasing smile in the mirror.

'Yeah, you do,' he agreed candidly. 'Let's see what
we can do to improve you. How about this for starters?'

His deft brown fingers dislodged her ridiculous, frilly
cap and pulled out her hairpins so that her heavy golden
hair tumbled in a thick mass on her shoulders. Josh
buried his face in it and nuzzled the back of her neck.
Then he inhaled deeply.

'Mmm, much better,' he said approvingly. 'Now what
about these awful clothes?'

Sliding his hands round her body, he spun her skil-
fully round to face him and then inspected her with a
grave expression. His gaze rested on the splash of tomato
purée on her apron and he clicked his tongue.

'What happened?' he asked. 'Did you have a life-threatening encounter with a dissatisfied customer?'

'No,' replied Penny. 'I had a life-threatening encounter with a plate of spaghetti bolognese. Josh, what are you doing?'

A note of alarm crept into her voice, for with a couple of deft movements, Josh had undone the strings of her apron and whisked the garment over her head. Worse still, he had now begun to unbutton the candy-striped dress. And, in spite of the delicious tremors this was sending through her entire body, Penny thought it was time to call a halt. Summoning up all her willpower, she pushed him away.

'Stop it, Josh!' she insisted.

He looked disappointed.

'I thought you wanted me to kiss every inch of your body,' he reminded her mockingly, trailing one finger sensually down the side of her throat.

She seized the finger and moved it firmly away.

'Maybe I do,' she replied coolly. 'But not yet. We've got things to talk about first. Josh, can't we sit down and have a drink somewhere?'

He shrugged.

'Whatever you like,' he said carelessly.

A dreadful pang of misgiving shot through her. If it hadn't been for Josh's unexpected announcement that he loved her, wild horses would not have dragged her here today. But after all, words were cheap. What if he had only said it so that he could seduce her? Tense with apprehension, she followed him through into the living-room and watched him suspiciously as he stopped in front of the cocktail cabinet.

'So what will you have to drink?' he asked.

'Just a Coke, thank you,' replied Penny stiffly.

'Sit down,' he invited. 'It won't take but a minute.'

She sat nervously at one end of a tartan-upholstered sofa and gazed around her. The living-room and kitchen were separated by a beige laminex counter that did double

duty as a breakfast bar. In the kitchen she could see
Josh moving about amid the gleaming appliances that
were found in so many American homes. A huge refrigerator with an ice-making tray, a wall oven, a food
processor, a complicated coffee machine. What a mar-
vellous place to cook, thought Penny enviously. I wish
I could try it some time. But that sent her thoughts skit-
tering anxiously around the topic of what her future relationship with Josh was likely to be, which made her
feel more apprehensive than ever. Hastily she withdrew
her attention to her immediate surroundings and realised
at once that the living-room bore the distinct imprint of
Josh's personality.

The furniture was uncompromisingly masculine and
yet stylish and casual at the same time. The dark red
and green tartan of the sofas was picked up by matching
curtains and scatter cushions, while there were a couple
of deep, inviting leather armchairs on either side of the
fireplace. Unexpectedly for midsummer, the fireplace was
piled with sawn pine logs, which gave off a rich, resinous
scent, and the plain white walls of the room were hung
with hunting prints and photos of deep-sea fishing. On
the antique cedar coffee table in front of Penny was a
scattering of farming journals and business magazines.
She gave a little start as Josh set down a large, ice-filled
Coke in front of her.

'What a nice living-room you've got!' she exclaimed
in a high, unnatural voice that sounded completely unlike
her own.

He looked at her in consternation.

'What the hell is the matter with you?' he demanded.

'N-nothing!' stammered Penny. 'I don't know what
you mean.'

He took a swift gulp of whisky from his own glass
and then set it down on the chimneypiece.

'Don't play games with me, Penny,' he said impatiently. 'You've been like a cat on hot bricks ever since

you sat down. What do you think I'm going to do? Fling
you on the bearskin rug and ravish you?'

She flung a swift, startled glance at the rug on the
polished floor and a quiver of mingled alarm and excitement shot through her. She blushed and lowered her
eyes.

'No, of course not,' she muttered.

'Don't think I'm not tempted,' murmured Josh
hoarsely. 'But when we reach that stage, I think we
should both know what we're getting into. You were quite
right to say we had things to talk about, Penny. So come
on, talk.'

Now that the moment had come, Penny found herself
surprisingly bereft of speech. Feeling like a wallflower
at a school dance, she clasped her hands nervously
around her Coke glass and smiled despairingly at him.

'What would you like to talk about?' she asked faintly.

'My heaven!' roared Josh, slamming his fist down on
the chimneypiece so that the whisky glass rattled. 'I lose
a whole damned week's work from the plantation
looking for you and then, when I find you, you act like
the village idiot! Where the hell were you anyway?'

Penny was still trying to take in the implication of
Josh's statement. A week's work? Had he really spent
the entire week looking for her?

'I-I was right here,' she stammered. 'Well, at Myrtle
Beach, anyway.'

'I figured that much out!' retorted Josh, striding impatiently across the room. 'Wilma Cox told me she'd
received a postcard from you with a Myrtle Beach
postmark, but no address. And there just happen to be
thousands of houses in this area. I even thought you
might be staying with Laney Cox, but I telephoned Laney
and she said she hadn't even seen you since the night of
the ball.'

'Laney said that?' demanded Penny with a break in
her voice.

In spite of Josh's furious expression, she had to fight down a bubble of laughter. But Josh was no fool. He heard the undertone of laughter and was across the room in three strides, gripping her by the shoulders.

'She was lying, wasn't she?' he insisted savagely. 'Damn it, you ought to be tarred and feathered, the pair of you! Don't you realise how irresponsible you were, running off like that?'

Penny's hackles rose.

'What do you mean—irresponsible?' she countered. 'What's so irresponsible about it?'

Josh gave an exasperated sigh.

'Haven't you been listening to me?' he snapped. 'I didn't know where the hell you were. It was just pure chance that I found you today when I did. You vanished out of my life without a word of explanation.'

'And what makes you feel that you were entitled to explanations of any kind?' seethed Penny. 'The last time I saw you, you had your arms wrapped around Brenda Sue Hartley, so I had pretty good grounds for thinking that you didn't care what I did!'

'That's ridiculous!' he growled. 'Of course I cared. And anyway, I didn't have my arms wrapped around Brenda Sue, she had her arms wrapped around me. There's a big difference!'

'Oh, is that so?' cooed Penny. 'Well, I'm afraid I didn't see it, and I still don't. It's perfectly clear to me that you only had two reasons for kissing me at Wilma Cox's party. One was to humiliate me and the other was to have your revenge on Brenda Sue.'

'That is the most absurd thing I have ever heard in my life!' scoffed Josh. 'Revenge? Revenge? I'm not interested in revenge. I couldn't give a damn about Brenda Sue any more!'

'Really?' asked Penny sweetly. 'Then what exactly were you doing with her in that pizza parlour today?'

His head came up and his jaw tightened.

'That's none of your damned business!' he replied through clenched teeth.

'Is that right?' demanded Penny. 'Now isn't that interesting? You're entitled to explanations about why I go away to the beach and where I stay, but I'm not entitled to any explanations about why you're seeing another woman, even though you claim to be in love with me! Some people would call that a double standard, Josh.'

'I can't help that,' replied Josh stubbornly. 'You'll just have to trust me, Penny.'

'Why should I?' stormed Penny. 'You know, Josh, I didn't realise until today just how incredibly arrogant you are! Which is pretty stupid of me, because your own housekeeper warned me.'

'Sarah McKendrick?' echoed Josh in a baffled voice.

'That's right!' agreed Penny. '"Never apologise, never explain—that's Mr Josh's way!" Those were practically the very first words she said to me, and I should have listened to her.'

Josh sighed and folded his arms. His granite features softened slightly as his gaze rested on her.

'Look, honey,' he said hesitantly, 'I know I'm not always the easiest guy in the world to get along with. Well, that's partly to do with the way I grew up. I was a hell-raiser when I was a teenager and my father was determined to beat it out of me. He thought the sun shone out of my brother Bruce, but every time I came home, he always got on my case right away. "Where have you been, what have you done, what trouble are you in now?" And if I gave him any back talk, he flattened me. I stood it until I was nineteen, then I lit out and joined the Air Force. Later on I put myself through college, and I guess I just grew out of my wildness anyhow. But one thing stayed with me from that time. I swore nobody else was ever going to make me give an account of myself like that again, and I've stuck to that.'

Penny's face had mirrored her shock and sympathy as Josh spoke of his troubled youth, but now she gave an exasperated sigh.

'I understand, Josh,' she said, laying a hand on his arm. 'But this is different. I don't want to keep worrying about what kind of man I've got myself involved with. I want to know what's going on between you and Brenda Sue!'

'Look, Penny,' he retorted warningly, 'lay off, will you? There are some things it's better not to know. Can't you just accept that?'

'No, I can't!' replied Penny mutinously. 'It makes me feel there's a really untrustworthy side to your nature. I can't help being uneasy about it.'

Josh gritted his teeth.

'Well, if it comes to that,' he pointed out, 'there are things in your nature that I can't help being uneasy about. Like your impulsiveness and irresponsibility and the way you're running through your inheritance at the rate of knots.'

She gasped indignantly.

'I should never have come here!' she snapped, jumping to her feet. 'You said you wanted to talk to me, but all you really want to do is insult me! If I want to run through my inheritance, I'll do it! It's my money, isn't it? And why shouldn't I want to live in my father's old home and follow in his footsteps a bit?'

'Well, you keep going the way you are,' advised Josh drily. 'William C. Eliot would be real proud of you.'

'And what's that supposed to mean?' demanded Penny hotly.

His face was suddenly shut and secretive.

'Nothing,' he said. 'Forget it.'

She could scarcely breathe with rage at the insult both to her father and herself. She gave him a slow, measuring look and antagonism welled up from the very soles of her shoes.

'You know what, Josh?' she said softly. 'I think that's the best idea you've suggested today. Let's forget everything. Especially the ridiculous idea that you and I should have any kind of relationship whatsoever!'

Josh's strong brown hand caught her wrist as she pushed past him.

'Is that all you've got to say to me?' he demanded furiously.

Penny choked back tears and realised that a strong smell of smoke was beginning to fill the room.

'No!' she snapped. 'I also want to tell you that your pizza is burning!'

And she slammed the door satisfyingly behind her.

Outside, the wind had grown stronger than ever and the sky was darkening ominously. A shiver of reaction passed through Penny's body and she stood gripping the railing on the wooden deck, wondering how on earth she was going to get back to Myrtle Beach. Down below she saw a convoy of cars gathered on the side of the road behind a black and white vehicle with a blue flashing light on its roof. A police car! Perhaps its driver could tell her where she could find a taxi to take her home.

Hurrying down the stairs, she ran across to the small knot of people who were gathered around the policeman. She saw that he was holding a megaphone to his lips, but the wind blew away his words. As he lowered the instrument, the people around him began to disperse. With a sudden twinge of anxiety, Penny hurried up to him.

'Excuse me, officer,' she begged. 'Can you tell me where I could find a taxi around here?'

He turned slowly round and she saw that he was a stocky, middle-aged man with a plum-coloured complexion and vivid blue eyes. His face wore a harassed expression.

'Where do you want to go, ma'am?' he asked.

'Myrtle Beach,' she replied.

He shook his head with a worried frown.

'You'd better not do that, ma'am,' he urged. 'We've just received a major hurricane warning and we're advising everybody to leave the coast and go inland as fast as they can. For your own safety, you should get out—now!'

CHAPTER SIX

'BUT I can't!' protested Penny in horror. 'My friend has gone fishing off Myrtle Beach. I can't just leave without checking that she's safe!'

'Well, you'd better make it snappy, ma'am,' advised the policeman. 'We got maybe three or fours hours before the hurricane hits, and it's gonna be a real lulu! Now, you say you need a ride back to Myrtle Beach?'

'Yes, sir,' agreed Penny unhappily.

'Well, maybe one of these good folk here can help you out,' said the policeman.

Picking up his megaphone, he strode back along the edge of the road, where two or three cars were still standing.

'Can any of you folks carry this lady to Myrtle Beach with you?' he boomed through the megaphone.

A balding man who was struggling to a tie a tarpaulin over his roof rack hailed Penny at once.

'Yes, ma'am. We're headed for Conway and we'd be happy to swing by Myrtle Beach and drop you off. Just climb in back with the kids.'

Before she had time to think, Penny found herself squashed in the back seat with two small boys and an assortment of rubber beach toys.

'Now, if you cain't find your friend right away, don't hang around,' warned the policeman. 'Get inland as fast as you can go! We're expecting waves eighteen feet high all along the Grand Strand, and there ain't no point in drownin'. Good luck now!'

He tapped a farewell on the window and then they were off into the gathering gloom. All the way to Myrtle Beach Penny's thoughts raged like the storm outside. Her first instinct on hearing the policeman's news had

106

been to rush straight back to the safety of Josh's arms.
But everything had happened so fast that there had been
little chance for that. And anyway, it wasn't as though
the hurricane changed anything. She still felt hurt by
Josh's insults, and a defiant glow of triumph burned
through her at the realisation that she had given him the
slip. All the same... wouldn't he be worried about her?
And what if he didn't hear the hurricane warnings and
was drowned or crushed by falling débris? Wouldn't it
be her fault for leaving him? Penny shuddered at the
thought. And how was she to find Laney amid all this
chaos? she wondered despairingly.

Yet at least one of her worries was soon settled, for
when they reached the Coxes' beach house the telephone
was ringing.

'You sure you're OK, honey?' asked the driver, as she
scrambled out of the car. 'You'd be real welcome to come
and stay with us at Conway.'

'I'll be fine now,' cried Penny gratefully, flying up the
stairs. 'Thank you so much! I must rush—that's
probably my friend!'

She inserted her key feverishly into the front door and
raced to the telephone.

'Laney?' she demanded anxiously.

'Yes! Oh, thank heavens you're there, Penny! I've
been trying to call you for the last hour. Hey, did you
hear the hurricane warnings?'

'Yes!' agreed Penny. 'Laney, where are you?'

'We put ashore at Carolina Beach and we're going to
drive inland from here. Listen, honey, can you take my
car and drive back home?'

'Sure,' agreed Penny with relief.

'OK, great. But don't stop to pack. There ain't nothin'
worth beans in that beach house anyway. And when you
get back, whatever you do, don't stay in your mobile
home—those places just get ripped apart in a hurricane.
Go to the closest big house—Waterford Hall or some
place like that. Got it?'

'OK,' agreed Penny. 'Bye, Laney. Good luck.'

With Laney's advice still ringing in her ears, she paused only to snatch up the canvas she had been working on all week and then hurried down to the car.

The drive back from the coast was a nightmare. Normally the trip only took an hour and half, but tonight the roads were snarled with traffic. Sudden gusts of wind buffeted the car and the headlights seemed to make little impression on the inky blackness that pressed down on the road. Unseen trees roared and threshed violently on either side of the highway and rain sluiced in furious gusts against the windows and doors. The radio crackled noisily, but from time to time news and weather reports came through with ominous clarity. 'Hurricane Janice is now generating winds of a hundred and ten miles per hour three hundred miles south-east of Charleston... The Governor has given orders for all coastal residents to evacuate their homes and move inland... If you are anywhere in the coastal region of the lower counties of South Carolina, leave immediately. We repeat, leave immediately!'

It was nearly four hours before Penny turned into a side road in Williamsburg County and saw the familiar avenue of live oaks caught in the beam of her headlights against the surrounding darkness. With a low gasp of relief, she headed up the gravel driveway towards the comforting bulk of Waterford Hall. So far she had been too preoccupied with driving to think much about Josh, but now a sudden uprush of feelings took her by surprise. She both dreaded and longed for the moment when he would come to the door and find her standing there. Unlike her, he hadn't had to make any detour to Myrtle Beach, so he must surely be home by now. Her imagination took a confused leap over the point where Josh apologised to her and settled happily on the moment where he swept her into his arms and crushed her. Thank goodness, I'm home! thought Penny. Then, slamming the car door, she raced up the steps to the front entrance.

The heat was overpowering, and before she had gone three paces, she was drenched by the buffeting rain. Steadying herself against the carved stone architrave of the door, she rang the brass doorbell. A light came on in the hall and the front door swung open. As it did so, a sudden gust of wind caught her in the small of the back and propelled her inside like a wave rider till she landed with a crash on a sturdy figure in front of her. A couple of bucketloads of rain drove in after them.

'Lawd have mercy!' cried Sarah McKendrick, clutching Penny's arms to steady both of them. 'If it ain't Miss Penny, safe and sound! Mr Josh must be so thankful to have you back!'

'Where is he?' asked Penny expectantly, looking hopefully into the interior of the house.

But the housekeeper was peering in quite a different direction. Clutching the heavy oak door to keep her balance, she was scanning the driving rain and darkness outside.

'Why, he's with you, ma'am,' she replied. 'Ain't he?'

Penny hunched herself against the furious gusts of wind that were devastating the entrance hall and set her full weight against the door, slamming it shut. Suddenly the uproar died down and there was a moment's stunned silence. Long enough for her to hear the panic-stricken thudding of her own heart.

'No, Sarah,' she said through stiff lips, 'he's not with me.'

The housekeeper gave a low, anxious gasp and her hand travelled up to cover her mouth.

'Well, you know where he is, then, don't you?' she demanded bitterly. 'He's out there in that storm...a-lookin' for you!'

Sarah was right about Josh's whereabouts. After his quarrel with Penny, he had rescued the incinerated pizzas and then hurried outside. But by the time he opened the

front door, Penny was already climbing into the car
bound for Myrtle Beach.

'Penny!' he shouted angrily. 'Penny! You come back
here!'

The only response was the loud revving of the car's
engine and the roar of waves on the beach.

'Oh, shoot!' exclaimed Josh furiously, and flung the
ruined pizzas over the edge of the deck.

They hit the ground in a flurry of sand, making the
policeman with the megaphone give a startled jump.

'I could pull you for littering, bud,' he grumbled,
looking down at the splattered remains. 'But I guess there
ain't much point, seein' the amount of litter that ole
hurricane will be leavin' here in a few hours' time.'

'Hurricane? What hurricane?' demanded Josh,
gripping the wooden railing.

The policeman waved his megaphone.

'Ain't you bin listenin'?' he complained. 'There's a
hurricane headed this way. The Governor wants everyone
evacuated.'

'Damn!' exclaimed Josh. 'Listen, Officer. Do you
know where that girl went? The one with the long blonde
hair that climbed into a car right in front of you?'

'Yeah, sure,' agreed the policeman. 'She said she was
goin' back home to Myrtle Beach to look for her friend.'

'Great!' exulted Josh, taking the stairs two at a time
and pausing at the bottom to pick up the mangled foil
trays and thrust them at the policeman. 'Here, have
yourself a pizza.'

'Thanks, buddy,' said the policeman with heavy irony
as Josh's BMW roared away down the road. 'I could
pull you for speeding too, but I guess there ain't much
use in that either.'

Yet in spite of Josh's impatience, the highway was so
thick with traffic that he could make little headway. He
found himself stuck behind a large lorry, and by the time
he reached the Coxes' beach house Penny had already
left. An impatient round of hammering on neighbours'

doors finally convinced him that she really had gone.
Defeated and anxious, he joined the long caravan of
traffic that was crawling inland in the driving rain. Like
Penny, he endured hours of nerve-racking driving in
steadily worsening weather, but unlike Penny he did not
head straight for Waterford Hall. When he reached the
side road leading away from Kingswood, he took the
track that led to Merivale.

By now he was thoroughly alarmed, although his fear
was not for himself but for Penny. He had lived through
one major hurricane already and knew the safety drills
as well as any man in the area. But Penny was a new-
comer, who might not recognise the torrential force of
the winds that were about to strike. She might already
be huddled in her glorified tin can of a home, believing
she was safe, when at any moment the hurricane could
rip it to shreds. After all, she had been stupid enough
to run off and leave him, even when she knew that a
hurricane was brewing. So she was probably stupid
enough to take refuge in a mobile home. Josh was conscious of an overwhelming urge to tan her hide. He was
also conscious of an overwhelming urge to crush her
against him and never let her go. But, as he rounded the
final curve of the sandy track that led to Merivale, all
thoughts of doing either vanished from his mind. For
with a sudden stupendous crash one of the huge Southern
pine trees slowly uprooted itself and lurched heavily down
towards Penny's trailer.

'No!' shouted Josh. 'No! No!'

He was out of the car and running before he even
realised what was happening. But it was already too late.
In the wavering beam from his pathetic little flashlight
he saw the metal walls of the trailer twist like soft drink
cans under the impact of the gigantic trunk. With a roar
of grief and outrage, he flung himself at the indifferent
mass of wood and beat on it with his fists.

'Penny!' he howled. 'Penny! Are you under there?
Answer me!'

*   *   *

Back at Waterford Hall, an anxious group was clustered
around the television set in the kitchen watching the latest
storm report. Against a background of palmetto trees
lashed by frenzied winds, they saw technicians struggling to repair the generator at a Charleston hospital.
Roaring black floodwaters were sweeping shoulder-high
around the men, but they battled doggedly on. At last,
exhausted but triumphant, they emerged to give the
cameramen a victory salute before staggering back inside
the hospital. Penny's throat swelled as she watched them
go.

'They're heroes, absolute heroes, going out in those
conditions,' she muttered.

'You're darn right,' agreed Sarah grimly, tearing
herself away from the television with a sigh. 'But they
ain't the only ones out there tryin' to save lives. There's
police and firefighters and emergency services folk. Not
to mention a lot of ordinary people caught up in the
middle of it all. Like Mr Josh.'

The grey-haired housekeeper closed her lips with a
snap, as if she had made a vow not to say any more, but
she could not resist shooting Penny a reproachful look.

'Now, don't take on so, Sarah,' soothed Gordon
McKendrick, patting his wife awkwardly on the shoulder.
'It ain't Miss Penny's fault the hurricane struck, nor it
ain't her fault that Mr Josh didn't make it back here.
Why, ten to one, he's just a-shelterin' in somebody's
house and you're worryin' yourself sick for nothin'. You
just keep busy, that's the thing to do.'

Penny bit her lip as the housekeeper pushed brusquely
by her to take up her place at the stove again. Gordon's
advice was sensible, but she could not help feeling that
Sarah had a point. In a muddled way, she did feel responsible for Josh's plight. Whichever way you looked
at it, it was really her doing. Even if Josh was an arrogant, overbearing swine, she should have swallowed
her pride and gone back to him at Pawleys Island. Then
he would never have gone looking for her and been

trapped in the storm. But if he died now, it would all
be her fault. The thought sent such a wave of misery
through her that she choked on a small dry sob. Sarah
looked at her sharply over the top of her bifocals.

'Now, don't you start!' she warned in exasperation.
'One of us frettin' about that man is quite enough. What
you need is somethin' to do that will take your mind off
him. Can you cook, Miss Penny?'

'Yes,' agreed Penny bleakly.

For the first time she became fully aware of the huge
array of rice steamers and deep-friers and broiling pans
that were bubbling furiously on Sarah's stove. It seemed
an odd time to go on a cooking spree, but she took the
bright floral apron that the older woman held out to her.

'Well then, you get cookin',' ordered Sarah. 'Last time
we had a hurricane in these parts, our electricity went
out for two weeks. I got me twenty-pounds of meat here
and I ain't aimin' to see it wasted.'

In the time that followed Penny obediently chopped
and stirred and ladled and basted. But the heady fragr-
ances of fried chicken, boiled corn, candied sweet potatoes and chocolate brownies that rose enticingly into
the air left her quite unmoved. There was room for only
one subject in her head, and that subject was Josh Miller.
She thought about the powerful, arrogant masculinity
of his body with its thick, dark hair and narrowed green
eyes, its craggy features and sensual mouth. She thought
about the mischievous charm of his rare smiles, the infuriating force of his personality, the breathtaking intensity of his lovemaking and the way her whole life
seemed to have exploded with colour and vitality ever
since he entered it. I love him, she thought with piercing
clarity. I love him so much that I couldn't bear to live
without him, however much he enrages me. Oh, let him
be safe! Please, please let him be safe!

'What was that?' demanded Penny sharply.

'What was what?' asked Sarah abstractedly, frowning
as she measured a cup of maize meal.

'I thought I heard something above the noise of the wind. A sort of swishing sound. A car, maybe?'

'I don't think so, honey. I didn't hear nothin'. Did you, Gordon?'

But Penny had already snatched off her apron, wiped her hands carelessly and hurried towards the kitchen door. Before she was even halfway there, the door swung open with a crash and a powerful figure strode in, soaked with rain and wild-eyed. He took one look at Penny, uttered a strangled roar of relief and swept her off the floor in a bone-cracking hug.

Hours seemed to pass as she laughed and cried and wept into his tangled dark hair. He was so wet that rain was running off him in puddles on to the floor, but she clung to him as if she would never let him go, gasping and protesting as he swung her exultantly from side to side. At last he set her down and her body slithered down into its proper place, firmly pressed against his. She gazed up at him through a blur of joyful tears.

'Oh, Josh,' she breathed, pressing her fingers deep into the satisfying hardness of his back. 'Oh, Josh!'

He took a long, slow breath, inhaling the fragrance of her hair, then tucked his chin firmly on to the top of her shining blonde head. His arms were locked rigidly around her back, forcing her body against him so hard that she could scarcely breathe.

'Marry me, Penny,' he ordered fiercely.

She gasped, but it was scarcely worth the effort, since he was holding her so tightly. Then his right hand shifted, catching her under the chin and turning her mouth up to his.

'W-what did you say?' she stammered as his lips covered hers.

It scarcely seemed to matter as he engulfed her in a kiss so deep that she thought she would drown. Her ears rang and fire surged through her veins as his mouth plundered hers. For a long, long moment, their bodies fused together and she felt an ecstatic sense of union and release. At last Josh's hold on her slackened and he spoke to her tenderly, punctuating his words with kisses that were no longer demanding, but swift and playful.

'I said—marry me—Penny,' he repeated.

Penny was stunned, but not half so stunned as Sarah McKendrick was a moment later. For when he had finished kissing Penny, Josh bent casually down and scooped her clear off the floor.

'Good evening, Sarah. Evening, Gordon,' he said cheerfully. 'You'll have to excuse us now. Miss Penny and me are going to bed.'

Then he strode across the kitchen and paused for a moment in the doorway, with Penny gasping and struggling in his arms.

'Oh, seein' as how you're cooking anyway,' he suggested, 'why don't you bake us a wedding cake while you're at it?'

'Josh, how could you?' protested Penny, scarlet with mortification as he set her down on the huge four-poster bed in his bedroom. 'Mrs McKendrick was shocked senseless!'

Josh gave a low growl of laughter.

'Well, I imagine she'll recover once we're safely married,' he said, turning her over and running one strong hand appreciatively over her hip. 'You know, you are one hell of a woman, Penny. Just thinking about touching you like this purely drives me crazy.'

She caught her breath uncertainly and put out a restraining hand to halt his caresses.

'Josh,' she murmured hesitantly, 'are you really asking me to marry you?'

He looked up, still wet and wild and dangerous-looking from his brush with the storm.

'Oh, no, Penny,' he replied with a long, devouring glance that made her body arch instinctively towards him, 'I'm not asking you anything—I'm telling you. You've got to marry me!'

'You high-handed brute!' protested Penny, as he lay down beside her and ran one hand lazily across her breasts. 'What makes you think I have to do anything that you tell me?'

Her nipples sprang into taut peaks under the tingling pressure of his fingers. She felt the low vibration of his laugh as he laid his cheek against her wet dress and nuzzled her slowly, provocatively.

'This,' he replied throatily, undoing one of her buttons and pressing his warm lips against her naked flesh. A second button followed. 'And this. The way you respond to me, the fact that you're my woman and you know it! Oh, hell, you've got gorgeous breasts, Penny. Like snowdrifts with rosebuds on top. I'm going to kiss them till you beg for mercy!'

She uttered a protesting whimper, as he undid another button and reached expertly for the fastening on her bra. There was a snapping sound, a muffled curse, then he hauled the dress roughly over her head. A moment later both bra and dress flew joyously through the air. With a sigh of anticipation, Josh lowered himself on to his elbow and ran his free hand exultantly down over her quivering flesh.

'Josh, stop it,' she murmured weakly, but his only answer was to take her nipple in his mouth and suck lingeringly on it.

'Ooh,' she moaned, tensing with delight. 'Oh, Josh, don't, don't...'

Her body was tingling with ripples of fire and a dark, pulsating heat was spreading from the innermost core of her being. Instinctively she caught her breath and clutched at his thick dark hair as his tongue went tantalisingly to work.

'Oh, Josh!' she breathed.

He raised his head.

'Do you want me to stop?' he demanded hoarsely.

'No, of course not!' she retorted in an anguished tone. 'I want you so badly I can't stand it any more!'

She heard his low growl of laughter, then suddenly he was hoisting himself up and kneeling on the bed. With swift, assured movements he stripped off his wet clothes and flung them on the floor, revealing his powerful naked body. Then he reached ruthlessly for her clinging silk briefs.

'I'm not wasting an invitation like that,' he murmured throatily, as he peeled them off. 'I love you, Penny, and I'm going to have you!'

She was half frightened by the dark, sensual passion in his eyes as he thrust her back on to the huge bed, but his strong hands were indescribably gentle as he picked up a stray tendril of her hair and brought it to his lips. Then he took a long, uneven breath and his grip tightened. Clenching his fists in her hair, he drew it into two bunches framing her face. His green eyes glinted like points of fire as he looked down into her wistful face.

'Oh, Penny,' he said through his teeth. 'You don't know what you do to me.'

Then he dragged her savagely against him and his mouth came down on hers, warm and fierce and urgent. There was no longer anything gentle about his love-making. Instead his body covered hers with a passion that both terrified and exhilarated her. She had known he was strong, but she had never imagined that the muscles in his arms were as hard as whipcords or that his back was like solid steel. He kissed her violently, forcing her lips apart and crushing her mouth with his. She should have been horrified, but instead she found an answering passion was blazing up inside her like a forest fire. Her hands tightened in his hair and she kissed him back with a raw, frenzied energy that made him groan with satisfaction. Squeezing her till her bones cracked, he brought her into close, urgent contact with his male body. She thrust herself against him, glorying in his primitive, masculine strength, the weight and power and savagery of his frame, the raw animal lust that pulsed through him. Together they rolled in a frenzy of kissing, gasping and straining together as if they were engaged in some furious contest. But at last Josh forced her into submission, thrusting her back against the lace pillows and holding her there, panting and struggling.

'Lie still,' he ordered. 'I told you I was going to kiss you till you begged for mercy.'

Her eyes were dilated with longing and her face was flushed, as he held her down.

'But, Josh, I want you now,' she whispered hoarsely. 'I'm ready for you.'

'Oh, no, you're not,' he murmured, trapping her wrists and gazing down at her with an expression that made her pulse with longing. 'I want you on fire before I take you, Penny. Now lie back and let me show you what I want from you.'

Thrills of ecstasy coursed through her body as he set to work. His lips and tongue and warm, deft fingers explored every crevice and hollow of her body, until she was writhing and groaning under his touch. With agonising skill he brought her again and again to the point of fulfilment, only to torment her by stopping. At last, when she was pleading shamelessly for relief, he took pity on her. Setting his mouth against her earlobe, he whispered into her ear. Even that was agony, for his warm breath sent trickles of excitement through her.

'Well, are you ready to beg for mercy?' he demanded hoarsely.

'Yes!' wailed Penny shamelessly, pressing herself against him and stroking the coarse, dark hair on his chest. 'Yes, you arrogant beast. Have mercy on me—please!'

He gave a low, satisfied chuckle and ran his hands tormentingly over her breasts.

'Are you sure you're ready?' he demanded lazily.

Penny's only response was a soft, exasperated moan. But it seemed to end Josh's iron control, for suddenly he abandoned all pretence of playing and caught her against him.

'I love you!' he said fiercely, kissing her closed eyelids.

Then he lowered himself on to her and drove in. Penny gave a gasp of satisfied longing, then her body pressed urgently against his, full of a timeless, aching need for release. Suddenly, overwhelmingly, Josh was hers. As he plunged deep inside her, a dark heat seemed to set every nerve in her body blazing. For a long time their bodies moved together in a rhythm as instinctive as breathing. At last Penny felt the throbbing insistence of her desire swell into an unbearable crescendo of delight. Her fingers dug convulsively into Josh's tense, muscular back and her lips parted softly as she gasped his name. She felt his powerful hands gripping her flesh and forcing her harder against him, then she heard his own harsh groan of fulfilment as he reached his climax. Rigid and shuddering, she collapsed against his shoulder and let out a deep, exultant sigh.

For a long time neither of them was capable of speech. And when she finally came back down to earth, she found the warm, heavy weight of Josh on top of her so pleasant that she was reluctant to move. He kissed her lazily on her closed eyelids.

'Am I crushing you?' he murmured.

'Mmm,' she agreed. 'But please don't stop.'

He laughed and ruffled her hair. Then he heaved himself free and lay beside her where he could gaze at her. His hand travelled caressingly down over her full breasts and slim waist.

'You know, I could get addicted to this,' he said, bending to drop a kiss on her throat.

'So could I,' she purred, snuggling against him.

He laughed and drew her against him. Then his green eyes grew suddenly sober as he looked down at her.

'I thought you were dead, Pen,' he said seriously. 'Just as I reached your house a pine tree fell on it and flattened it. I practically went berserk, thinking you were inside, until I realised that I hadn't seen any lights before the tree fell.'

'What?' exclaimed Penny in horror, sitting up and clutching the sheet around her. 'You mean my house is ruined?'

'Yeah, I'm afraid so,' agreed Josh ruefully. 'Not that it really matters, when you think how tacky the place was. I would have pulled it down anyway once we were married and used the land for raising gladioli.'

There was a sudden deafening silence. For the first time in an hour or so, Penny noticed the roar of the storm overhead. Then she took a deep breath and counted to ten.

'Oh, would you just?' she said softly.

'Sure,' agreed Josh, lying back with his hands locked behind his head. 'We could have sold the mobile home to somebody and had it hauled away. As it is now, we'll just have to clear out the rubble. But I'll still be able to plant a good field of gladioli on the site and pump water up from the river for them. They should do fine right there.'

'I see,' said Penny frostily. 'You don't think you ought to ask my opinion about doing any of this, I suppose?'

'Well, of course not, honey,' he replied mildly. 'You may be terrific in bed, but you don't know beans when it comes to farming. So why the hell would I ask your opinion about it?'

Penny ground her teeth.

'Because it just happens to be my land and my house!' she hissed. 'And you don't care a damn about that. You didn't even tell me the house was ruined until now!'

Josh shrugged impatiently.

'I didn't think it mattered all that much,' he replied. 'Once I found out you were safe, that was all that counted. And when we got upstairs I had other things on my mind.'

'Yes, of course you did!' she agreed, her eyes filling with angry tears. 'All you were interested in was getting me into bed. You couldn't even be bothered telling me that I'd just lost everything I possessed!'

'Penny!' shouted Josh, sitting bolt upright and clutching her by the shoulders. 'What the hell are you carrying on about? You haven't lost a damned thing! That trailer was insured, and all it had in it were a few things you bought in some five-and-dime store. So why in blazes do you have to act like you got driven out of your ancestral home and I'm the wicked landlord with the whip?'

'Because that's the way you make me feel!' retorted Penny furiously. 'Ever since I first arrived here, you've been trying to get that piece of land away from me. I'm starting to wonder if you proposed to me just so you could get your hands on it!'

'Oh, come on!' roared Josh. 'That is the most pea-brained suggestion I've heard in my entire life. Ten acres of overgrown swamp and I'm supposed to be signing away my freedom just so I can get hold of it! Now you listen to me and you listen good, Penny. The only reason I want that land is because I hate to see it go back to swamp when it could be fertile and productive. And why do you want to keep it, anyway? It was only sentimental claptrap about good old William C. Eliot that stopped you from selling it to me in the first place. That and pure cussedness. I tell you, Penny, if I could drop a bomb on that piece of land and blow it away, I sure as hell would! All it's ever done is come between us.'

Penny's mouth set in a tight, offended line.

'You know something?' she demanded. 'I don't think it's just Merivale that comes between us, Josh. I think it's my father. Every time you mention his name, you have a sneer in your voice. I know you quarrelled with him over the sale of Waterford Hall, but why do you hate him so much? What happened between you?'

Josh loosened his grip on her shoulders and folded his arms stubbornly.

'Nothing that concerns you,' he replied airily. 'I don't intend to discuss it, Penny, so don't bother asking.'

With a wail of frustration she picked up her pillow
and hit him on the head with it.

'There you go again!' she cried. 'It's not fair, Josh!
You're so damned secretive. Why won't you tell me
anything?'

'Because I don't want you to know,' he replied with
maddening smugness. 'And don't hit me with pillows
unless you want a counter-attack. Like this!'

The counter-attack was so blissful that Penny soon
found herself giggling and squirming in Josh's iron grip.
While they were still grappling and laughing, there was
a sudden thunderous crash overhead and the lights went
out. Penny gave a frightened gasp and found herself
crushed against Josh's powerful chest with his arms
tightly around her. He stroked her hair soothingly and
she could feel the strong, steady thudding of his heart
beneath her cheek.

'Don't be frightened, honey,' he urged in his deep,
resonant voice. 'I guess the power cables have gone
down, but whatever happens, I'll see you safely through
it. That applies to the hurricane and everything else. All
you got to do is trust me.'

But long after he had gone to sleep, Penny lay awake,
staring into the thick, heavy darkness. Overhead the
hurricane still roared out of control, but it was nothing
to the turmoil in her own mind. Josh had told her that
he loved her and wanted to marry her, tonight they had
actually become lovers and here he was lying beside her,
warm and solid and breathing deeply. She should have
been floating on a cloud of ecstasy, but she could not
subdue the sense of uneasiness that flooded through her.
Somehow she kept seeing Brenda Sue in the pizza parlour
with one hand laid possessively on Josh's arm. Of course,
he had told Penny that all she had to do was trust him.
But could she?

CHAPTER SEVEN

'Ok, rise and shine. We got work to do, honey.'

Penny groaned and burrowed into the pillows, but Josh was nothing if not ruthless. Seizing the covers with one hand, he stripped them off the bed in a single swoop, leaving her naked and shocked.

'Oh, you beast!' she exclaimed, yawning and sitting up.

The glint in his eyes made her gasp and cover her breasts with her hands as memory flooded back to her.

'It's kind of late for that, isn't it?' asked Josh in a mocking voice. 'Besides, I was enjoying the view.'

Penny dived for the end of the bed, seized the corner of the sheet and hauled it up towards her. Only when she was tucked primly underneath it did she condescend to reply.

'That's unfair,' she pointed out. 'You're fully dressed. It puts me at a disadvantage.'

Josh was wearing an open-necked white shirt and a pair of acid-wash Levi jeans that showed the muscular outline of his thighs. With his tanned skin and the hint of dark stubble on his face he looked more like a pirate than ever. As he bent to kiss her, his chin grated her like sandpaper.

'Ow!' she complained. 'Aren't you shaving today?'

'Nope,' he replied, but his voice was sober. 'There's too much to do, sugar. We've got to go see how much damage the hurricane caused.'

Penny winced.

'Do you know, I forgot all about it for a moment,' she admitted. 'It's so hard to believe it ever happened, with the sun pouring in the window like that.'

She gestured to the open window where the white lace curtains were billowing in a gentle breeze.

'I know,' agreed Josh heavily. 'But it's real all right. I've been out for a quick look, and it's not a pretty sight. The telephone is out, the power lines are down, the water supply is cut and there are enough trees flattened to keep a pulp mill in business for six months. But what I'm really worried about are the people. I got me a hundred employees and I want to know that they're safe and their families are OK. Plus all the old folks and little kids in these parts. I thought I'd take the four-wheel-drive out and have a look round. You want to come?'

'Yes, of course,' agreed Penny swiftly. 'But, Josh, how will you get through? Won't the roads be blocked by fallen trees?'

'Yes, ma'am,' he replied without hesitation. 'But I'll take a chainsaw and cut my way through if I have to.'

His face was so determined that Penny quailed. She had often complained about Josh's high-handed, arrogant manner, but perhaps there were times when a masterful temperament was useful. Yet it was unsettling to witness this sudden transformation in his manner. All the passionate intimacy of the previous night had suddenly vanished, and the man who was now sitting on the edge of the bed seemed like a brisk, practical stranger. She felt a weird sense of unreality as he patted her absentmindedly on the knee and then took a notepad and pen out of his breast pocket.

'Now, let's see,' he murmured thoughtfully. 'I told Sarah to bring you some breakfast and clean clothes. As soon as you're ready, we'll get moving. I got a list of things a mile long here that we'll need to check.'

It hardly seemed like the right moment to ask Josh to discuss their wedding plans, and, in any case, he soon rose to his feet and strode out of the room. When Penny arrived downstairs ten minutes later, dressed and fed, he summoned her into the kitchen with a shrill whistle.

'In here, honey. We're just getting sorted out.'

He and Gordon McKendrick were both poring over a map which was laid out in the centre of the large kitchen table, and Sarah was up to her elbows in suds at the sink. Penny set down her breakfast tray and unloaded the dishes into the water.

'Thank you, Sarah,' she said appreciatively. 'The coffee and the bacon were delicious. I don't know how you managed it under these conditions.'

'Hmph!' snorted Sarah. 'Well, it ain't easy keepin' house with the kind of goin's on we had here last night, but I do my best.'

Penny caught Josh's slow wink and had to stifle a giggle. She wasn't at all sure that Sarah was referring to the hurricane, and she decided the wisest course was to beat a hasty retreat. Pulling out a chair, she sat down beside Josh.

'What's happening?' she asked.

'Things are pretty much under control here at the house,' he replied. 'After Hurricane Hugo a couple of years back, I had this place pretty well fitted out in case of another disaster. We've got a large rainwater tank out in back, so we'll be fine for drinking water until the regular supply is reconnected. Plus I've hooked up the generator from my motor home so the electricity can be fed back into the house. Of course, I pulled the main-breaker first—I don't want to electrocute the repairmen when they finally get out here. So now I guess we'd better hit the road and see how our neighbours are getting on. McKendrick, you take the pick-up truck and head west along the Clarksville Road, and Penny and I will go north towards Kingswood. Take the CB radio and keep in close touch with me. Tell any of our men who are fit to work that I want them here at the Hall for an emergency meeting at six o'clock tonight. All plantation work is to stop until further notice. I want every man-Jack of those guys helping the emergency services until this County is back on its feet.'

'Got it!' agreed Gordon.

Josh folded the map and headed briskly for the back door so that Penny had to run to keep up with him. As they emerged on to the brick-paved driveway at the rear of the house, she gave an involuntary gasp of dismay.

'Oh, no!' she breathed. 'I don't believe it!'

Josh smiled grimly.

'I know,' he agreed. 'And we're the lucky ones, believe it or not. There'll be places far worse hit than this.'

Penny shuddered as she surveyed the devastation. It was as if a particularly malicious giant had thrown a temper tantrum and rampaged through the fields like a destructive child. Trees were uprooted or snapped off halfway down their trunks. The smokehouse roof was smashed in and one of the garden sheds had been ripped off its foundations and flung against a fence. But the most awe-inspiring sight of all was the gigantic live oak tree at the end of the avenue, which had been torn up by the roots and now lay wedged immovably across the main entrance to Waterford Hall. Josh stood staring at it for a moment with an unreadable expression on his face and then clicked his tongue.

'Hell!' he said indifferently. 'I guess there's no use standing around here like a fool when I could be doing something useful. But there's no way I can get past that baby today. We'll have to take the track down past your place, Penny, and just hope it's clear.'

It was clear, apart from a single fallen pine tree, which barely halted Josh for two minutes.

'Stay here,' he ordered.

Then, snatching up his chainsaw, he sprang out of the vehicle and attacked the fallen tree. Penny covered her ears to shut out the loud whine of the saw as it bit deep into the wood. To her astonishment, she saw that Josh was almost smiling as he worked. The muscles on his arms stood out like taut steel cables under his tanned skin and he moved at the speed of light. The moment he had cut through one end of the trunk, he sprang lithely across the track and set to work on the other. Moments

later there was a muffled thud as the section of wood
fell to the ground. Josh put the chainsaw away, hauled
the wood to one side of the track and then climbed back
into the vehicle, smelling of sweat and pine resin.

'One down, five thousand to go,' he muttered grimly.
'But at least I feel as if we're getting somewhere now.
Right, next stop Merivale.'

Penny was not prepared for the flood of emotion that
swept through her when she saw her home crumpled
under the weight of a large pine tree. Of course, there
was a shaky feeling of relief and gratitude that she hadn't
been inside, but there were also smaller, more foolish
feelings. A sense of anger at the futility of it all, outrage
at the thought that she had just finished decorating the
place, regret at the loss of her possessions. She wasn't
aware that these thoughts showed quite clearly in her
face, so it took her by surprise when Josh squeezed her
shoulder.

'Do you want to go take a look?' he asked.

'No,' she sighed. 'There may be people trapped somewhere needing help. That's much more important than
anything I've lost.'

'That's my girl!' he said approvingly, and put his foot
on the accelerator.

Yet, although his impatience was obvious in the way
he tensed forward and gripped the steering-wheel, he
drove carefully, scanning the road ahead for obstacles
and urging Penny to keep her eyes open.

'Look out for downed electric wires,' he warned. 'And
any low spots that might be flooded. But most of all,
watch out for distress signals—people waving bits of
clothing, that kind of thing.'

They had gone only another half-mile or so when
Penny let out a yelp.

'Over there!' she cried. 'It looks like a cabin or something, but the front wall is ripped away. I can see a little
boy standing on the grass, but no sign of any adults.'

Josh turned the vehicle up the rough track, and they both winced at the sight that met their eyes. The entire front portion of a cabin had been sheared away so that the interior looked like a stage set of a house with one wall removed. As they came to a halt, a black boy of about six came running towards them.

'Well, hi there, Tommy,' said Josh, crouching down to the child's level.

The small figure hurtled into his arms and dissolved in a storm of incoherent sobs and complaints.

'Hey, c'mon now,' urged Josh. 'A big guy like you doesn't need to cry like that. You're not hurt, are you, Tommy?'

'No, sir,' gulped Tommy. 'But my daddy, he didn't come home last night and there was this big crash and half the house, it blowed right away. And Mama, she just won't move, Mr Josh. I tell her "Mama, that baby is cryin', you got to do somethin'," but she don't listen, she don't say nothin'. I don't know what to do!'

Penny's heart went cold with dread at this desperate plea, but Josh was already striding swiftly towards the ruined house. As they came closer, they heard the angry, frantic wails of a desperate infant and the exasperated voice of an older child trying to hush it. Picking his way through the rubble of a ruined front porch and a shattered wall, Josh came to a halt in the centre of what had once been a living-room. Penny followed his gaze and saw a woman of thirty or so, sitting at a table with her head buried in her hands. She was so still that for a moment Penny thought she had actually been killed where she sat, until she saw the slow rise and fall of her breast as she breathed. Josh laid his hand comfortingly on the woman's shoulder and a convulsive shudder went through her.

'I'm a God-fearin' woman, Mr Miller,' she said in a dull monotone. 'I don't drink or smoke or cuss and I go to church reg'lar. So why did this happen to me? My man Moses didn't come home last night, and that ain't

like him. He's dead, ain't he? Is that what you came to
tell me?'

Josh let out his breath in a long sigh.

'Penny, see what you can do for the baby, will you?'
he urged. 'I've got to try and help this lady.'

What Josh said Penny never found out, for she was
too busy changing the baby's nappy, reassuring the
frightened older sister and brother and bringing basic
supplies from the back of the four-wheel-drive. But
whatever it was, it must have penetrated the poor
woman's daze, for when they left ten minutes later, she
was wielding a broom amid the wreckage. And the two
older children were happily chewing on licorice whips
and waving vigorously.

'Packets of candy!' exclaimed Penny, shaking her head
admiringly. 'I knew you'd brought emergency supplies
with you, Josh, but I didn't know you were that well
organised!'

Josh grinned.

'I told Sarah to buy in everything people would need,'
he said with a shrug. 'I guess she's the one who's well
organised, not me.'

Yet as the day wore on, Penny realised that Josh's
modest claim was not strictly true. It became more and
more apparent with every visit they made that he was
tough, resourceful and a source of inspiration to people
around him. All through the long, hot day, he drove
himself relentlessly on, cutting a path with the chainsaw
through huge branches, driving injured people to hospital and distributing emergency supplies. And, even
when they returned home, he did no more than snatch
a quick wash and change of clothes before hurrying
downstairs to organise the disaster relief meeting. Penny
followed more slowly with a subdued expression on her
face. Of course she was proud of Josh, but it seemed
cruel that they could not spend more time together just
when they had fallen in love. It was as if the hurricane
had brought them together only to split them apart again.

That thought came back to her many times in the weeks that followed the disaster. Everybody in the County seemed to be working immensely hard to repair the damage, but nobody worked harder than Josh. When Penny woke in the mornings at six o'clock, he was already up and on the road, distributing food and water, fixing tarpaulins over ruined buildings or acting as an advisor to the Army and the Red Cross. He rarely appeared on time for dinner, and when he did, he would gulp his food in silence and disappear again. And it was generally after midnight when he finally climbed into bed. Not that the fiery passion that drew them together had abated one bit. Far from it. Penny frequently woke to find herself being ruthlessly swept into an embrace that left her gasping and whimpering with delight. But their lovemaking at this time was fierce, hot-blooded and brief. And when it was over, Josh was usually asleep before his head hit the pillow. There was never any time for the slow ripening of intimacy, the delicious hours of aimless talk.

Penny did her best to accept this. She told herself that Josh had a job to do and she would be childish to resent it. And she tried to help in any way she could. Along with Laney and Sarah McKendrick and half a dozen volunteers, she set up a meals on wheels service, operating out of Waterford Hall. Many homes had been devastated by the hurricane and most were still without electricity two weeks later, so the two girls were a welcome sight as they drove around the back roads with their containers of fried chicken and steaming vegetables. Yet, unlike Josh, Penny was not a human dynamo with unlimited energy. After three weeks of gruelling work in a humid climate, she was feeling exhausted, resentful and ready to flare up at the slightest provocation. And, Josh being Josh, the provocation was not long in coming.

One evening she decided to make a supreme effort to entice him to spend an hour or two in her company. She told Sarah to have an evening off and, after extracting a promise from Josh that he would be home for dinner by eight o'clock, she set to work in the kitchen. In spite of three weeks spent churning out and serving mass meals, it was surprisingly good fun to plan an intimate dinner for two. Penny found herself humming cheerfully as she leafed through Sarah's cookbooks to choose the menu. Shrimp cocktail on a bed of shredded lettuce, roast duck with black cherry sauce, creamed potatoes and vegetables and, the pièce de résistance, a delectable lemon soufflé. Although Josh had sworn piously that he would be back at eight on the dot, Penny had little faith in his promises, so she had chosen the dishes carefully. The shrimp could be prepared ahead of time and stored in the refrigerator, the duck would be forgiving if the main course were a little late and only the soufflé demanded exact timing. But Penny didn't intend to start cooking that until she had Josh firmly captive in a dining chair. With one eye on the clock, she flitted happily round the kitchen, and soon the delicious smell of roasting duck filled the air. Drying her hands on her apron, she dashed into the dining-room, set the table with a damask tablecloth, gleaming silver and slender white candles and then hurried upstairs to take a quick shower.

When eight o'clock arrived, she was sitting on a brocade sofa in the small sitting-room wearing a flowing peach chiffon dress and a welcoming smile. By eight-thirty the smile had become a little forced, and by eighty forty-three, when Josh strode in, it had been replaced by a thunderous scowl.

'Hi, honey,' he said, kissing her on the cheek. 'When do we eat?'

'Forty-three minutes ago,' replied Penny in a taut voice.

'Say what?' he demanded.

'Oh, never mind,' she snapped. 'Go and sit in the dining-room. I'll bring in the first course.'

When she arrived with the two shrimp cocktails shortly after, Josh was sitting in his place at the head of the table with a pile of folders propped dangerously close to the candles and a printed report open on the table in front of him. With an exasperated sigh, Penny set down his shrimp cocktail and pointedly moved the folders on to a side table.

'What are you doing that for?' he demanded. 'They're not in my way.'

'No, but they're in my way,' retorted Penny shortly, lighting the candles. 'Besides, they might catch fire.'

'Well, do we really need the candles?' objected Josh. 'We're not having company or anything, are we?'

She caught her breath and counted slowly to ten.

'No, we are not having company,' she replied, sitting in her own place and shaking out her napkin.

'Good,' said Josh with relief. Then he picked up the printed report again. 'This shrimp looks mighty tasty. Tell Sarah she did a good job, won't you?'

And he turned a page and began to read. Penny gave a low wail of annoyance.

'Do you have to do that?' she demanded.

'Do what?' he asked innocently without looking up.

'Read! I thought just for once we might talk tonight.'

'Sure, honey,' agreed Josh amiably, pushing the report aside, but leaving it craftily open so that he could still see it. 'What do you want to talk about?'

'Oh, don't bother if you've got better things to do,' replied Penny in a voice dripping with sarcasm. 'I can see you're dying to get back to that report.'

'Well, yeah, I am really,' he agreed. 'Thanks, honey.'

And he immediately bent his head again. From that point on, the meal went from bad to worse. It was true that Josh showed his appreciation of the roast duck by eating two large helpings of it, but while doing so he read aloud extracts from the Red Cross report, which did little to soothe Penny's ruffled feelings. But the final disaster did not arrive until the moment when she lifted

the soufflé dish triumphantly out of the oven and carried
it briskly into the dining-room. It was a dream of a
soufflé, light, fluffy and creaming over the top of the
dish in a delicately browned cloud, while the tangy lemon
aroma was enough to set anybody's mouth watering. Just
let Josh read while he's eating this! thought Penny, as
she slid the silver serving spoon into the hot, quivering
mass. If this doesn't make him sit up and take notice,
nothing will. She slid the portions efficiently on to the
waiting plates, set Josh's helping in front of him and sat
smiling proudly with her spoon poised. At that moment
the telephone rang.

'Excuse me,' said Josh.

He was gone for ten minutes. Long enough for the
soufflé to subside like a collapsed balloon on his plate.
When he returned, it was looking pale and limp and full
of pathos—rather like Penny.

'That was Jimmy Walton,' explained Josh. 'Now that
we've got things more or less under control near
Kingswood, he wants to know if I'll join the Grantlyville
Disaster Relief Committee. Of course, it means I won't
be at home as much as I am right now, but they were
pretty hard hit by the hurricane. I guess I ought to do
it. What do you think, honey?'

'I think,' said Penny slowly and clearly, 'that if you
say the word "hurricane" again, I am going to scream
violently and run from the room.'

Josh stared at her, aghast. He even closed the Red
Cross report.

'What's the matter, honey?' he demanded.

But to her dismay, she found that she could make no
rational reply. She opened her mouth twice, only to find
that tears were prickling under her eyelids. Biting her
clenched fist, she gazed despairingly across the table at
Josh. At last she found her voice.

'My soufflé's ruined,' she whispered shakily.

His face cleared.

'Is that all?' he said with relief. 'Hell, honey, that don't matter. I don't even like soufflé.'

Penny burst into tears. There was a long, confused moment when she was dimly aware of the candles blurring against the shadowy background of the room, of Josh striding swiftly towards her, of tears rolling down her cheeks and splashing on the white tablecloth. Then his arms came round her and he held her safe and warm against his powerful masculine body.

'What is this, honey?' he demanded.

But all she could do was to sob out her feelings of exhaustion and defeat, while he stroked her hair and crooned to her. At last she drew a long, gulping breath and accepted the handkerchief he held out to her. Fiercely she scrubbed at her red eyes and blew her nose.

'You never want to spend any time with me,' she complained in a wobbly voice. 'You'd rather do anything than be with me.'

'Hey now, that's not true!' protested Josh. 'I don't want to be parted from you, sweetheart. It's just that everything has been so frantic ever since the hurricane. And don't you scream because I said that word.'

Penny gave a tremulous smile.

'But if you don't want to be parted from me,' she demanded, 'why are you thinking of joining the Grantlyville Committee? They must have able-bodied men of their own over there. All right, maybe in the first couple of weeks, you couldn't help being away. But, as you say, things are more or less under control here now. The electricity's back on, the water's back on, people are all getting on with their lives again. All except us. I'm beginning to think I'd have more chance of seeing you if I were a Red Cross worker or some disaster victim from thirty miles away.'

A wry smile spread over his face.

'So that's it, is it?' he demanded. 'You want more of my time and attention?'

'Yes,' choked Penny.

'You little idiot,' murmured Josh affectionately, stroking her tumbled hair and then turning her face up to his. 'I thought you knew that I loved you. I told you the night of the hurricane.'

'And that's supposed to last me for the next fifty years, is it?' retorted Penny with a touch of spirit.

She felt rather than heard his low growl of laughter.

'Well, I guess I could tell you again, if you're real desperate,' he conceded, stroking one finger along the line of her jaw.

'I'm real desperate,' she replied in her best Southern drawl.

He kissed her slowly and appreciatively on her open mouth.

'I love you, Penny,' he said simply. 'But you never should have doubted it. OK, maybe I've been away from dawn to dusk and even longer, but that was because I had work to do. And I never stopped thinking about you.'

'Truly?' she whispered huskily.

'Truly,' insisted Josh. 'In fact, the thought of you kept me going. Some of those houses were really wrecked bad, Penny, and I'm not kidding. I've seen homes that the hurricane just picked up in one piece and dumped down somewhere else, with half their rooms smashed to pieces. But when I was out there knee-deep in dirty water, with gnats biting me and the heat enough to broil you alive, I kept thinking about you. And I'd say to myself, ''I'm doing this for Penny. This place is her future now, as well as mine.'' I tell you, honey, some days that was the only thing that kept me going.'

'Oh, Josh!' exclaimed Penny remorsefully. 'I'm sorry—I didn't mean to be so selfish. It's just that I was starting to think you really didn't care about me at all and that it was only the chaos of the hurricane that flung us together.'

'Well, quit thinking it right now!' he ordered. 'Hell,
Penny, if you're going to get dumb ideas like that in
your head, I'm going to have to do something about it.'

His face moved closer to hers, so close that she could
feel the rasp of his unshaven skin against hers and see
the sensual gleam in his narrowed green eyes. A sudden,
delicious tremor of arousal tingled through her.

'Such as?' she demanded mockingly, arching her body
so that her breasts brushed against his thin shirt.

He caught his breath and swallowed.

'Such as telling the guys in Grantlyville they'll have
to manage without me,' he muttered without ever taking
his eyes off the gentle swell of her breasts. 'And such as
taking you down to Charleston for a few days' rest and
recreation leave. And, of course, I'll have to give you a
re-education programme to change your attitudes.'

His deft fingers found the zip at the back of her dress
and skimmed it swiftly down. A moment later her bra
fell softly to the floor on top of the dress. Then Josh
fell to his knees and buried his face joyfully in her warm
breasts.

'Starting now,' he said.

The next morning Penny came bounding out of the front
door of the house as soon as she heard the BMW on the
gravel driveway. As usual, Josh had risen before she was
even awake, but this time he had obviously not been out
clearing débris or delivering supplies. Instead he sat
behind the wheel looking suave and relaxed. His hair
was neatly combed, his face was shaven, and in place of
the awful old jeans and torn shirts that had been his
uniform for the past three weeks he wore stylish grey
slacks, a crisp grey and blue shirt and leather penny
loafers. With a sly grin, he climbed out of the car and
sauntered up the steps to meet Penny.

'Did you have a good night, dear?' he asked
solicitously.

She flushed crimson with embarrassment.

'Josh!' she hissed furiously, casting a swift glance around to see if Sarah was within earshot.

'It's all right,' he soothed. 'She's busy in the laundry. Now, give me those suitcases and we'll get moving.'

While he was stowing the suitcases briskly in the back of the car, Penny came slowly down the stairs, frowning over her shopping list.

'Well, have you written down everything we need to buy and do?' asked Josh.

'I think so,' she agreed. 'New clothes for me. All mine were in my trailer when it was wrecked and I've been wearing Laney's for the last three weeks. Various items from the hardware store for you. See the insurance company about sending an assessor to look at my mobile home. Visit the art gallery down near the Battery, because Laney says the woman who owns it might buy some of my watercolours. And have some fun.'

'That sounds like a good agenda,' said Josh approvingly. 'Well, let's go!'

Penny paused with one hand on the door of the car, as her gaze travelled down the sweeping green lawn in front of them. In the centre of it was a large, heart-shaped flower-bed, which had been ruined in the hurricane when a tree fell across it. Although the tree had been hauled away, the flowers beneath it now lay smashed and withered.

'Could we get some more flowers for that heart-shaped bed too?' she asked. 'I've always thought it was so pretty with the red and white balsam in the middle of the blue ageratums around the outside.'

'Yeah, sure,' agreed Josh, as she climbed in. 'You know, there's a story about that flower-bed, which might appeal to you. Most women seem to like it, although I can't really see why.'

'What is it?' she asked, intrigued.

'Well, apparently your great-great...I don't know how many greats—six or seven, I guess—your great-great-great-great-great-great-grandfather, Captain Thomas

Eliot, was the guy who built this house back in 1792. Anyway, when he came out here with his wife to check the boundaries before the building got started, he dug his heel into the soil and traced out that heart-shaped bed. And he said it must stay like that as a sign that there'd always be love in this house.'

'Oh, Josh, that's a wonderful story!' cried Penny, twisting in her seat for a final view of the beautiful red brick house at the end of its avenue of live oaks. 'And it's all the more reason for replanting the flower-bed properly. Are those the kind of flowers they had then, do you know?'

He shrugged comically.

'Hell, how would I know?' he retorted. 'All I can tell you is that there've been flowers like that in that bed every summer since I first saw the place. But it's no good twisting my arm for the historical details. I'm not real interested in that kind of thing.'

Penny sighed.

'Oh, men!' she exclaimed in disgust. 'I think it's amazing that my ancestors lived in this place for nearly two hundred years and now I'm here, carrying the torch. I only wish my father could be here to share it with me.'

Josh was silent for a moment, gripping the steering-wheel and staring grimly down the road ahead.

'Well, maybe,' he said at last. 'But personally I don't set much store by ancestors. In my view it's what you are yourself that counts. Anyway, tell me more about that last item on your list. Having fun. Now I figure we ought to paint the town red when we reach Charleston!'

They did paint the town red. Although Charleston had been very hard hit by the hurricane, three weeks of gruelling work by its citizens had cleared up the worst of the mess, and it was still a remarkably beautiful city. Josh had booked a suite in a gracious old house on Meeting Street which had been converted into a private hotel, and from this elegant base they went out determined to enjoy themselves. The first day was given over to business. Penny filled in a pile of forms in the insurance office and was told that an assessor would soon come to visit her, Josh bought cartons full of hardware and together they stormed the art galleries of the city with Penny's portfolio of watercolours. When the owner of the fourth gallery they visited bought two of her paintings and even suggested an exhibition at Christmas, Penny was ecstatic. After that there was no question of doing anything but celebrating. And they could hardly have found a better place than Charleston for that. They rode around the city in a horse-drawn surrey, admiring the gracious colonnaded houses with their gardens full of palmetto trees and scarlet oleanders, they cruised on the vast blue-grey stretch of the harbour where pirates had once sailed, they shopped for handwoven baskets in the old Slave Mart, and at night they ate and danced and held hands in the soft light of restaurants and nightclubs. Penny had never had so much fun packed into a five-day period before, and it was not until the last day that any friction occurred between her and Josh.

They were strolling on the South Battery, that point of land which jutted out into the blue water of the harbour and caught the breezes, where the most beautiful homes in the city were located. Penny was dawdling along, exclaiming delightedly about all the little features that were only noticed during a leisurely walk. Two carved stone pineapples topping a pair of gateposts, purple wistaria cascading over a pergola, fire hydrants painted to resemble little soldiers with scarlet coats and blue trousers, a horse-drawn carriage with red wheels and a fringed roof on top, a young boy with a fishing pole. But Josh didn't seem to share her pleasure in any of these discoveries. In fact, the closer they got to the end of the Battery, the more uneasy he seemed to be.

'I think we should be heading back now,' he said determinedly. 'I wouldn't be a mite surprised if that insurance assessor shows up at your place this afternoon.'

'I doubt it,' replied Penny drily. 'Oh, Josh, look! See
that big house over there with the colonnade? It's got a
heart-shaped flower-bed in front, just like Waterford
Hall! I must go and take a look.'

And before he could stop her, she darted across the
road and peered eagerly through the iron railings of the
fence. There was a black gardener at work in the flower-
bed and, seeing her interested gaze, he straightened up
and touched his hat to her.

'Afternoon, ma'am,' he said politely. 'Mighty pretty
flowers, ain't they?'

At that moment Josh appeared beside her, and the
gardener's smile widened into a delighted grin.

'Why, Mr Josh!' he drawled. 'Well, I'll be darned!
It's good to see you, sir. What are you doin' down in
these parts?'

Josh's face took on a hunted look.

'It's good to see you too, Leroy,' he replied. 'This is
my fiancée, Penny Owen. Leroy is a local man from
round Clarksville, Penny.'

'Fiancée!' exclaimed Leroy, savouring the word. 'You
don't say! Well, why don't you go inside and see Mr
Richard, sir? I'm sure he'd be mighty proud to drink
your health, and Miss Penny's too.'

'Thanks, Leroy,' said Josh, taking Penny's arm, 'but
we've got to run. Penny's expecting the insurance assessor this afternoon to check on the hurricane damage
to her house, so we'll have to get moving.'

'Why, sure,' agreed Leroy, clutching his spade. 'You
want to catch him while you can, ma'am. They're so
busy after this hurricane, he might not get back to you
for six months if you ain't home when he calls. Well,
goodbye, then. Y'all take care now.'

Penny looked at Josh with a puzzled frown as he
marched her briskly back along the Battery.

'What was all that about?' she demanded. 'And who
is Richard anyway?'

Josh looked harassed.

'He's a lawyer,' he said hurriedly, dragging her across the road almost under the wheels of one of the horse-drawn carriages. 'Originally he came from Williamsburg County, but he's been living in Charleston for over twenty years now. I've had occasional dealings with him. He's a real nice fellow.'

'Then why didn't you want to go and have a drink with him?' persisted Penny.

Josh gave an exasperated sigh.

'Because I want to get you back to Merivale in case the insurance assessor shows up this afternoon,' he replied.

'But that's ridiculous!' she protested, as he found the car and bundled her into it with obvious relief. 'It was never a firm appointment. They only said they might send somebody out late Friday afternoon. They didn't even mention a definite time. Besides, I would have liked to meet Richard and see inside that beautiful house.'

Josh was already busy buckling up his seatbelt and turning the key in the ignition. His mouth set in the line that she recognised as a sign of sheer, inflexible obstinacy.

'Well, that's tough!' he said carelessly. 'Because I think we should get moving.'

'It's absurd,' she muttered in an annoyed voice. 'I'll bet the insurance assessor won't even be there.'

But that was just where she was wrong. For, when they turned into the road that led to Merivale, they saw a shiny red car parked in the long driveway that led to the wreck of her mobile home. On its side in large letters were the words 'Monarch Insurance Company Incorporated.'

'Well, hey, look at that!' exclaimed Josh in a voice that combined triumph and surprise.

'I see it!' retorted Penny, feeling more annoyed than pleased.

Josh brought the car to a halt on the roadside verge.

'Honey, Leroy's right,' he said firmly. 'If you don't catch that guy today, he may not get back here for

another six months. Why don't you go on down and
show him the damage? I want to drop these boxes of
hardware up at the big house, but I'll come and join
you as soon as I can.'

'All right,' she agreed reluctantly. 'But what do I say
to him?'

'You don't need to say anything. Just show him what
happened. It'll probably be old Ted Quilty, and he's a
capable man. He'll know what to do.'

But it wasn't any kind of man, capable or otherwise,
who met Penny's gaze when she came hurrying down
the last stretch of the driveway. The figure who turned
slowly around with a large tape measure in one hand
was unmistakably a woman—and a glamorous one at
that. Her dark hair was combed into sleek, ruffled waves,
framing an exquisitely made up face. Her eyes were a
deep indigo blue and she wore a crisp blue suit with a
metallic sheen to it that glittered in the sunlight. And
her Cupid's bow lips were parted in a dazzling smile.

'Well, hello there,' said Brenda Sue.

CHAPTER EIGHT

FOR ONE agonised moment Penny wished she could be teleported right off the face of the planet. The last person she had expected to see outside her mobile home was Josh's former girlfriend, but when she blinked twice in rapid succession the vision remained. It was Brenda Sue, no question of that. Not only that, but her smile was fixed firmly in place and her hand outstretched. Gingerly Penny stepped forward and shook the long, tense fingers tipped with scarlet nails.

'Hello,' she muttered uneasily. 'Whatever are you doing here?'

Brenda gave a low ripple of laughter.

'Why, honey!' she exclaimed. 'We're so busy with all the claims following that awful hurricane, just about everybody's been sent out into the field. Usually I work in the office at Kingswood, but I've been in the business ever since I left high school, and what I don't know about it ain't worth two bits. Why, I used to tag along with my daddy on assessment visits when I was no more than knee-high to a grasshopper! So don't you worry none, I can handle all the damage in the world for you.'

Penny couldn't help feeling that there was a slightly ominous ring to that statement, but she gave a sickly smile and tagged along after Brenda Sue as the other girl marched briskly across the lawn. Surprisingly, Brenda Sue's claims to efficiency seemed to be well founded. She took photos and measurements, fired rapid lists of questions about the fittings in the trailer, and finally closed her notebook with a snap.

'Well, you shouldn't have no trouble gettin' your money,' she said brightly. 'So I'll be movin' along in a

minute. But before I go, there's somethin' I want to talk
to you about.'

Penny was conscious of a queasy feeling in the pit of
her stomach. Here it comes, she thought desperately.
She's going to take me apart for stealing Josh from her.
Longingly she glanced up the track which led from
Merivale to Waterford Hall, but there was no sign of
rescue. And Brenda Sue was settling herself gracefully
into a stone garden bench which had miraculously escaped the ravages of the hurricane and smiling invitingly
at her.

'Come sit by me and we'll talk,' she urged, patting
the bench.

Feeling rather as if she were going visiting in an alli-
gator pit, Penny sat down.

'Look, if it's about Josh——' she began.

But she was interrupted by another of Brenda Sue's
silvery trills of laughter.

'Oh, honey, it ain't about Josh!' she protested. 'Well,
shoot, I was gettin' kind of tired of him anyways, and
I ain't the kind of girl to bear a grudge. No, it's about
somethin' else.'

There was a pause while she fished in her soft leather
handbag and drew out a silver cigarette case and lighter.

'You smoke?' she asked.

'No, thanks,' replied Penny, gazing at her warily but
conscious of a mounting curiosity.

She had to hold her curiosity in check while Brenda
Sue drew out a cigarette, set it delicately between her
red lips and flicked the lighter. Only when she had inhaled deeply and blown out a long cloud of blue smoke
did she arch her dark eyebrows and smile tantalisingly
at Penny.

'Well now,' she murmured, 'I hear you've been pretty
busy yourself since the hurricane. I believe you've been
doin' some meals on wheels work, is that right?'

'Yes,' replied Penny, puzzled.

'You didn't by any chance come across an old lady name of Louella McGregor, lives by herself in a little white house at the far end of Burns?'

'No, I don't think so,' said Penny, frowning. 'Oh, wait, though. Not that old lady of ninety-two that's supposed to have a perfectly preserved 1932 Oldsmobile in her garage?'

'Yes, ma'am, that's the one.'

'Well, I never actually met her myself,' admitted Penny. 'I was supposed to take a meal to her one day, but Josh wanted me to do something else, so he asked Laney to go instead. But why do you ask about her?'

Brenda Sue examined the backs of her shapely red nails complacently.

'Oh, it's just that I was talking to her only a few days ago. She had some windows blown out in the hurricane and I was checkin' on the damage. And from what she said, she's mighty keen to meet you.'

'To meet me!' exclaimed Penny. 'But why?'

Brenda Sue smiled.

'Well, I did hear tell that you were William Eliot's daughter,' she confided. 'Is that true?'

'Yes,' agreed Penny, still looking bewildered.

'Well, there you are, then,' said Brenda Sue with the air of a magician wrapping up a difficult trick. 'Old Louella McGregor was an Eliot before she married. In fact, from what she said, she was your granddaddy's aunt, and she knew your daddy real well too. She's got a whole bunch of old photo albums and such that she wants to show you.'

'Really?' exclaimed Penny, unable to suppress her sudden rush of interest and excitement. 'Well, thank you for letting me know.'

'You're welcome,' replied Brenda Sue, rising to her feet. 'Mind now, if you go to visit her, it might be better not to mention it to Josh. He couldn't abide your daddy, for some reason, although I doubt if that was William

C's fault. Josh can be mighty pigheaded about some things.'

Penny gave a non-committal murmur. Privately she was inclined to agree with Brenda Sue, but she certainly wasn't going to be drawn into discussing Josh's short-comings with the other girl.

'Well, look who's here!' exclaimed Brenda Sue brightly, dropping her unfinished cigarette to the ground and grinding it underfoot. 'If it ain't the man himself!'

Penny glanced up, startled, and saw a figure striding down the last stretch of the sandy track. It was Josh with his hands thrust deep into his pockets, his body tensed forward and his face as black as thunder.

'Well, hey, Josh!' trilled Brenda Sue. 'How ya doin'?'

He ignored her outstretched hand.

'What are you doing here, Brenda Sue?' he demanded in an unfriendly voice.

Brenda Sue pouted prettily.

'Is that any way to treat an old friend?' she com-plained. 'Why, I'm here to check Miss Penny's trailer, Josh, and assess the damages.'

'Let me see,' ordered Josh, stretching out his hand for her notebook.

'Well, I ain't really supposed to show that to nobody,' protested Brenda Sue. 'But since it's you, Josh, I guess you can take an itty-bitty look at it.'

He scarcely listened to her. He was frowning thought-fully down at the notes in her book.

'That all seems to be in order,' he admitted at last, closing the notebook and handing it back. 'But why are you working as an assessor, Brenda Sue? I thought you were on the office staff.'

Her eyes were suddenly as round as marbles.

'Well, I am, honey,' she agreed. 'But they just cain't get enough people to handle the workload right now, and when I heard that y'all needed somebody out here, I decided to do you a favour and come out myself.'

'That's mighty generous of you,' said Josh sceptically.

'Well, thanks, sugar,' cooed Brenda Sue, reaching out
and patting him on the cheek. 'And is that true what I
hear down at the post office that you and Penny are
getting married come springtime?'

He gave a sardonic grin and wrapped one powerful
arm around Penny's shoulders.

'Actually, I wasn't aware that Betty Anne Summers
had chosen a date for us,' he admitted. 'But apart from
that, it's pretty accurate. And I guess the spring would
be as good as any other time.'

'Spring, huh?' mused Brenda Sue, and suddenly her
deep blue eyes were not so much like marbles as like
spheres of ice. 'Well, a lot can happen in seven months,
but I wish you all the happiness you deserve, Josh. And
you, Penny.'

She gave them a low, semi-circular wave, as if she were
practising a dance routine, then minced gracefully across
to her car. Silently Josh opened the door for her and
Brenda Sue climbed in with a movement that left her
long, shapely leg extended for several seconds beneath
his gaze.

'Why, thank you, sugar!' she purred. 'Bye-bye,
Penny!'

As the car disappeared down the drive, Penny stole a
glance at Josh, wondering if he had noticed that slender
ankle and high-heeled shoe so provocatively displayed.
He had.

'Lord, that woman's a bitch!' he marvelled, shaking
his head. 'I can't believe I didn't wake up to her sooner.'

Penny relaxed, feeling suddenly relieved. In fact, she
decided she could afford to be generous. Slipping her
arm around his waist, she rubbed her cheek affectionately against his shoulder.

'Oh, she's not so bad,' she said carelessly. 'And she
was really quite helpful about the insurance claim.'

Josh looked down at her with a thoughtful frown.

'I don't know,' he growled, rubbing his chin.
'Whenever she's as nice as pie like that, she's generally

up to something. What was she talking to you about on
the garden bench? Was it just the insurance claim?'

Penny hesitated. For an instant she wanted to share
the exciting news about her newly discovered relative with
Josh. But something held her back. It was pretty obvious that there had been some bitter dispute between
Josh and William Eliot. So what would he say if she
told him she intended to ask the old woman about her
father? Wouldn't he just forbid her to go? The mere
thought made her blaze with indignation, and suddenly
she made up her mind.

'Yes,' she agreed crisply, 'that's all.'

Josh still looked suspicious, so Penny decided to
change the subject.

'Do you really want a spring wedding?' she asked,
nestling closer to him.

He closed his hand over hers and smiled down at her
with indulgent warmth.

'Honey, if it were left up to me,' he said with
amusement, 'I'd suggest a Justice of the Peace and a
couple of witnesses in about a month's time. But I have
a feeling you'd like to make a bit more of a splash than
that. Like a white lace wedding dress and a big bouquet
that you could throw to Laney Cox. And two hundred
people in their most uncomfortable clothes sitting down
to dinner in the ballroom and making speeches. And
your mama boohooing into a handkerchief about losing
her little girl and my mama congratulating herself on
the purty silver tea service she'd given us. Isn't that
right?'

Penny gasped with laughter and punched his arm.

'You wretch!' she complained. 'You make it sound
utterly hideous!'

'It is hideous,' agreed Josh tranquilly. 'Totally and
utterly hideous. But I'd even go through that to know
that you were really mine, Penny. And I think you're
going to be the most beautiful bride Waterford Hall has
ever seen, standing out here in your white lace dress with

the dogwoods in bloom all around you. Just like a troupe
of pink and white bridesmaids.'

'Oh, Josh,' murmured Penny shakily. 'Do you really?'

'Yes,' he said simply.

And he drew her into his arms and kissed her with a
hungry intensity that made her heart thud and her breath
come deeply and slowly. When at last he released her,
she felt as dizzy and elated as if she had just stepped off
a carousel.

'I love you,' she murmured with a catch in her voice.

'Well, in that case, let's get back to the house and
start drawing up the guest list,' said Josh practically.
'And I guess we'd better phone our families and break
the news too. Your mother would be home by now,
wouldn't she?'

Startled, Penny looked at the date on her wristwatch.

'The fifth of September,' she said slowly. 'I can't believe the time has gone so fast. Yes, I suppose she would.'

But to her disappointment, her mother's phone rang
and rang without any answer. However, Josh's mother
was at home and in fine form. For the first five minutes
after hearing the news, she could manage nothing more
than a litany of 'Gracious!', 'Mercy!' and 'I declare!',
but after that she rallied and demanded to have Penny
put on the line. Josh, who had been holding the receiver
at arm's length while his mother exclaimed and marvelled, handed it over with relief. And then it was Penny's
turn to be interrogated about her family, complimented
on her darling accent and quizzed about her china pattern
and the number of silver teaspoons she owned. With
Josh rolling his eyes and sipping imaginary cups of tea
in the background, this was quite an ordeal, and it was
a great relief to Penny when the call finally ended.

'Whew!' she exclaimed. 'I'm beginning to think you're
right. The register office looks better and better by the
minute.'

'Great!' said Josh, rubbing his hands. 'Want me to
arrange it, then?'

'Don't you dare!' retorted Penny. 'Even if I haven't the faintest idea what my china pattern is, I want a proper wedding.'

'Well, I'm going to be real busy with the gladiolus fields come springtime,' pointed out Josh craftily. 'I might not even have time for a honeymoon then.'

'Oh, Josh!' wailed Penny.

He relented.

'Well, maybe I could manage a week in the Bahamas,' he conceded. 'Provided McKendrick isn't going to be away. Maybe I ought to tell him about it now, so he doesn't plan to take his vacation then.'

Dropping a swift kiss on the top of her head, he strode away in the direction of the barn. Left alone, Penny glanced stealthily around, then hurried upstairs to the privacy of the bedroom she shared with Josh to make yet another telephone call. Her hands were shaking as she dialled the number. At any moment Josh or Sarah might innocently pick up the telephone downstairs and overhear her. The thought made her feel oddly furtive, as if she were planning a bank robbery and might be discovered. But fortunately, after only four rings, her call was answered.

'Hello,' said a quavering voice.

'Hello. My name is Penny Owen. Am I speaking to——'

'You'll have to speak up! I'm hard of hearing.'

'Am I speaking to Mrs Louella McGregor?' demanded Penny, thinking how difficult it was to shout and whisper at the same time.

'Yes, I'm Louella McGregor. Are you the nurse who's comin' to listen to my heart? Now, it's been beatin' real fast, and every time I spend an hour or so out in the garden diggin', it purely bangs like a drum. Why, I believe I've had a heart attack every mornin' this week, and I just cain't work the way I used to——'

'Excuse me,' cut in Penny desperately, speaking as clearly as she could. 'I'm not the nurse, I'm William Eliot's daughter. I was told that——'

It was her turn to be interrupted.

'Young Billy's daughter!' cried Louella rapturously. 'Well, my land, why didn't you say so, honey? I've been expectin' you to call all week. I even baked some chocolate chip cookies for you, so you'd better drop by tomorrow morning before they're too stale to eat. I'll see you round ten o'clock.'

Penny blinked as the line suddenly went dead. Talking to Louella McGregor was a disconcerting exercise, but once she grasped the issue she certainly came straight to the point. If only she were equally straightforward when it came to discussing Penny's father... A smile of anticipation spread over Penny's face. Well, whether Josh liked it or not, perhaps she was finally going to discover the truth about his feud with her father.

Next morning at ten o'clock she pulled up outside a neat white cottage about five miles from Waterford Hall. She was driving the pick-up truck which she had used for her meals on wheels visits, and on the seat beside her she had a wicker basket containing a bunch of flowers from the conservatory at Waterford Hall and a box of soft-centre chocolates. As she climbed out of the vehicle and walked towards the house, she gazed around her with interest. Evidently Louella had been lucky in the hurricane. A small wooden outhouse had overturned and lay drunkenly against the side fence, and a pine tree had blown down, but most of the wood from this was already split and stacked. Apart from this, there was little sign of damage.

Louella was sitting on the front porch in a grey rocking chair, shelling peas and rocking, but as Penny came up the path she rose to her feet and set down the basin.

'Well, hey,' she said, folding Penny into a scrawny but pleasantly scented embrace. 'You must be Billy Eliot's daughter.'

'Yes, ma'am,' agreed Penny, slipping into Southern speech.

She kissed the old woman's wrinkled, papery cheek and gazed steadily back into her keen, silvery-grey eyes.

'Hmph!' snorted Louella suspiciously. 'You don't look much like an Eliot to me.'

'I take after my mother,' explained Penny with a grin.

Fortunately the grin did more good than the explanation.

'Well, my land!' exclaimed the old woman. 'Now, when you smiled just for a moment there, you looked the image of your daddy. He always had a dimple like that too.'

'Did he?' asked Penny shyly.

'Why, sure, honey! Don't you remember?'

Penny was just opening her mouth to explain that she had never met her father, when Louella plumped herself down in the rocking chair again, pumped vigorously like a child gaining height on a swing and gestured at her wood heap.

'Well, what do you think of my log pile?' she demanded abruptly. 'Purty, ain't it? One of them young GI's split those logs for me.'

'The soldiers have done some wonderful work since the hurricane,' agreed Penny sincerely.

'Yes, ma'am,' said Louella firmly. 'Mind now, we've got President Eisenhower to thank for that. The minute the storm was over, he called in the troops to help.'

The unwelcome suspicion dawned on Penny that Louella was wandering in her mind. Hadn't Eisenhower been President during the big hurricane in 1954? She set the chocolates and flowers down on the table next to Louella and cleared her throat, uncertain where to begin.

'Well, sit down, honey,' urged Louella, rocking vigorously. 'Now tell me, where did you do your nursing training? In Columbia?'

Penny sighed.

'I'm not the nurse,' she reminded the old woman
gently. 'I'm William Eliot's daughter. Do you remember
William Eliot?'

For a moment the keen grey eyes clouded, then suddenly Louella's face cleared.

'I'm sorry, honey,' she said with a touch of embarrassment, 'I guess I'm gettin' old and kind of forgetful.
But if you're Billy's daughter, you'll be wantin' to see
them old photo albums, won't you?'

'Yes, please,' agreed Penny with relief.

Louella picked up the flowers and sniffed them.

'Now, that's mighty thoughtful of you, honey,' she
said. 'Come inside and help me find a vase and then
we'll have some cookies together.'

Stepping into the dim coolness inside, Penny reflected
that Louella's vagueness did not seem to hinder her
housekeeping ability in any way. The room smelled of
furniture polish and fresh flowers, and once Penny's eyes
grew accustomed to the light she saw that it was very
well kept. The Wedgwood plates in the china cabinet
gleamed through the shining glass doors, patchwork
cushions in bright floral prints were plumped up in the
corners of the sofa and every surface carried an array
of family photos in silver frames. In the centre of the
room a sleek tabby cat lay snoozing on a rag rug. As
the hinges squealed protestingly on the wire door, the
cat opened one eye, yowled and slunk out of the room.

'He don't like visitors,' explained Louella serenely.
'Don't you take no notice of him, honey. Just come
through to the dining-room and we'll set a while and
take some tea.'

As she held the swing door open for Penny with one
hand, Louella casually reached out and seized a framed
photograph from the top of the china cupboard.

'Now that's your daddy,' she said with satisfaction.

With a low cry of delight, Penny sat down at the mahogany dining-table and gazed raptly at the photo. For
the first time in her life, she saw her father clearly. She

scarcely breathed as she took in the details of crisp, wavy black hair, deep blue eyes, a heart-stoppingly attractive smile and a quirky dimple in one cheek. It was easy to see how her mother had fallen in love with this man. She gazed and gazed in silence.

'He's very handsome,' she murmured at last.

'Yes, ma'am,' agreed Louella, setting a pitch of iced tea and a plate of cookies on a serving mat in front of her. 'Now that photo was taken when he was about twenty-five, just before he went to Australia. But right from the time he was born, he was good-lookin' like that. Why, he was the cutest baby I ever did see. And, my, was he a charmer! No matter what bad things he did, his mama always had to forgive him. He'd look at her with his purty smile and she just couldn't stay mad at him. Now, will you have some iced tea, honey?'

The iced tea was strong and sweet and tangy with lemon. Penny drank two glasses and ate three of the cookies, which were equally delicious, thick and sticky and crammed full of chopped nuts and lumps of melted chocolate.

'Oh, that was wonderful!' she sighed. 'Thank you, Mrs McGregor.'

'You're welcome, honey. Well, I bet they don't feed you so good in that nursing home, do they? But you call me Louella. Now where were we?'

'You were going to tell me about my father. William Eliot,' prompted Penny gently.

'Oh, yes,' agreed Louella. 'I'll bring out the photo albums and show you.'

With trembling hands she loaded the empty glasses and plates on to a tray and Penny carried it into the kitchen. When she returned, Louella was sitting at the table with a stack of photo albums open in front of her, polishing her spectacles. She smiled warmly and opened the first album. Penny noticed that her hands were thin and clawlike and the skin was stretched tightly over them like parchment.

'This is your daddy when he was a baby,' Louella said fondly. 'And that's your grandmama Grace and your grandaddy Bob. Bob was my brother Harry's son and I was always real fond of him, seein' as how I was never blessed with any children of my own. Don't he look handsome in his Army uniform? He was killed in action in Normandy, poor man.'

'Oh, I am sorry,' murmured Penny warmly, as the old woman sighed over this long-ago grief. 'Is that why my father was an only child?'

'Land sakes, honey!' exclaimed Louella, rallying. 'Whatever put a notion like that into your head? Why, Billy wasn't an only child! No, ma'am. There was his brother Richard too. Now he warn't nearly such a pretty child as your daddy, but he was a fine boy in his way, real smart at his books and always top of the class.'

Penny blinked at this revelation of another unsuspected relative.

'What happened to him?' she asked curiously. 'Did he die?'

'Gracious, no!' exclaimed Louella with a touch of impatience. 'He's alive and well and livin' in Charleston with a wife and two children.'

Penny's mouth fell open.

'You mean... I've got an uncle in Charleston?' she said slowly. 'But that's incredible! I can't believe nobody told me about it before.'

Louella shrugged.

'They've probably forgotten all about him,' she replied. 'Richard ain't hardly set foot in Williamsburg County since he left to go to law school when he was nineteen. Never even came to visit his mama, God rest her soul. And that's real strange when you think about it, because he used to worship the ground she trod. And he was real attached to Waterford Hall too. Why, you know that big heart-shaped flower bed right in front of the house? Somebody told me Richard had one made just like it outside his house in Charleston.'

Penny felt a curious sick feeling in her stomach, as if
she had suddenly plunged ten floors in a lift. She cleared
her throat.

'Whereabouts in Charleston does Richard live?' she
asked, but even as she spoke, she knew the answer.

'Why, right on the Battery, honey,' replied Louella
with a touch of pride. 'He's a real successful attorney
and he's got a fine big house there. It's strange you ain't
never been to visit him. But maybe after all these years
nobody in Williamsburg County even remembered he
was there.'

Penny shook her head in a dazed fashion. Louella was
wrong. Only yesterday morning Josh Miller had known
perfectly well that her uncle lived on the Battery! Not
only that, but he had taken damned good care that she
should not find out.

'Josh Miller knows!' she exclaimed bitterly.

Louella's face darkened.

'Well, he would!' she retorted in an angry, tremulous
voice. 'Goodness knows, he had plenty of dealings with
Richard Eliot ten years ago. Why, your daddy would
never have had to sell Waterford Hall to Josh Miller if
Miller hadn't turned Richard against him!'

'What do you mean?' demanded Penny, aghast.
'Whatever happened?'

Louella's withered face worked with emotion.

'I near heard of anything so shameful in my life,' she
said at last. 'The plantation was left to your daddy, with
a life interest to your grandmama. Now your daddy spent
most of his life in foreign parts, and, according to what
folks say, he made some real unlucky business invest-
ments. Well, about ten years ago he needed to borrow
money, so he took out a mortgage on Waterford Hall
with Josh Miller. But the next thing we knew Josh Miller
called in the mortgage and said your daddy would either
have to pay up or get out. Why, I believe that nearly
broke Billy's heart. He tried to get his brother Richard
to lend him the money, but Josh Miller managed to turn

Richard against him. And in the end he forced your daddy to sell, although he didn't pay him anything like what the place was really worth.'

'But that's dreadful!' exclaimed Penny, appalled. 'How could Josh do such a thing?'

'Well, he did,' affirmed Louella. 'And I reckon your daddy was right. Josh Miller was nothin' but a lowdown, greedy rattlesnake of a man, who didn't care about nobody but himself. Where are you goin', honey?'

For Penny had risen to her feet and was standing with her hands clenching and unclenching on the back of her chair and her breath coming in painful gulps.

'I'm sorry, Louella,' she exclaimed. 'You were really kind to give me the tea and show me the photos, but I must go. There's somebody I have to see!'

She found Josh sitting in the study at Waterford Hall doing the monthly accounts. The computer screen was flickering brightly and there were shoeboxes full of bills and receipts laid out on the floor. In the middle of this organised chaos sat Josh, gulping coffee and frowning at a calculator. In his acid-wash jeans and casual mint sports shirt, he looked the picture of innocence and normality.

'Hi, honey,' he murmured, looking up with the quirky grin that normally made Penny's heart turn over. 'How are things?'

An incredulous rage surged up in her breast. How dared Josh sit there drinking coffee and smiling at her as if nothing had happened, when her whole world had just come to an end?

'Don't you "Hi, honey" me!' she retorted grimly, advancing towards him.

Josh rose to his feet, looking mildly alarmed.

'Now hold it right there, sugar,' he urged with the air of a man placating a savage dog. 'Don't step on that box. It's got all my Internal Revenue receipts filed in order, and it took me two hours to get it that way.'

'Damn the Internal Revenue Service!' shouted Penny, and she kicked the box furiously out of her way.

A snowstorm of papers fluttered into the air and then gently subsided. Josh let out a roar of fury and pounced. Penny backed hastily away behind a free-standing occasional table, but Josh cleared the table in a lithe vault and lifted her clear off the floor.

'What the hell do you think you're doing?' he shouted.

His green eyes blazed and the muscles in his neck stood out like whipcords as he held her in the air like a rag doll. But her face was just as fierce and outraged as his.

'Why didn't you tell me I had an uncle living in Charleston?' she hissed.

There was a sudden electrifying silence. She heard the swift rasp of Josh's breathing and felt the sudden tremor of shock that ran through his powerful arms as he held her above him. Then slowly he lowered her on to the Persian carpet.

'You've been talking to Louella McGregor,' he said softly.

'Yes!' snapped Penny.

He gave an exasperated sigh. Penny was reminded of the morning after the hurricane when he had found a massive pine tree blocking his path and coolly set to work to demolish the inconvenient obstacle. Turning his back on her, he walked across to the desk and shut off the computer. She only noticed its high-pitched whine as the screen information vanished. Then Josh stood facing her, cool and silent and watchful.

'Well, who told you to go there?' he demanded at last.

Penny was disconcerted. This wasn't the way she had expected the conversation to go, with Josh firing questions at her as if she were a criminal in the dock. Damn it, he was the one in the wrong, not her! So why should she feel suddenly at a loss?

'Brenda Sue Hartley,' she replied, tossing her head.

Josh gave a mirthless laugh.

'Damn her time!' he exclaimed savagely. 'I knew she was cooking up some kind of trouble.'

And he sat down and began shovelling the scattered papers back into their box.

'Well, aren't you going to say anything?' demanded Penny aggressively.

He shrugged.

'What do you want me to say?' he retorted indifferently.

'Well, you hid my uncle's existence from me, didn't you?' cried Penny with a touch of hysteria. 'Do you deny it?'

He sighed again, as if he were annoyed by her persistence.

'No, I don't deny it,' he said wearily. 'So you might as well sit down. There's no need for you to go buzzing around like a demented mosquito.'

'Mosquito?' she echoed indignantly. 'You've got a nerve, Josh Miller! You pull an underhanded stunt like that on me and then all you can do is make fun of me!'

Josh winced and ran his fingers through his thick dark hair.

'I'm not making fun of you, Penny,' he muttered. 'I just wish you'd drop the whole subject.'

Penny snorted.

'I'll bet you do!' she retorted venomously. 'Just like the way you wished I'd drop the subject when I saw you at Myrtle Beach with Brenda Sue. And I was actually fool enough to do it too! But this time you're not getting off so easily, Josh Miller! This time I want some answers.'

Josh sighed and set a pile of papers unsteadily on the computer desk. As he stacked them, his lean, craggy face wore an unreadable expression. Then suddenly he darted her a swift, assessing glance like a fencer sizing up an opponent.

'Well, what do you want to know?' he asked coolly.

Penny padded warily across to the desk and glared at him.

'To begin with, I want to know why you didn't tell me that Richard Eliot existed,' she challenged.

He shrugged.

'I judged that it was better for you not to be acquainted with him,' he replied arrogantly.

She spluttered.

'I'll choose my own acquaintances, thank you very much!' she snapped furiously.

And with her teeth clenched in pure rage, she slammed both fists down on the computer desk. Josh's pile of papers lurched drunkenly and cascaded to the floor.

'Oh, shoot!' he groaned.

'Leave them there!' snapped Penny. 'Leave them there and look at me, damn you! All right, supposing I pass over the breathtaking arrogance of your assumption that you have any right to choose my friends and acquaintances, kindly tell me this! Why on earth did you "judge that it was better" for me not to be acquainted with Richard Eliot?'

Josh looked shifty, but he stood his ground.

'That's my business,' he said stubbornly, folding his arms and thrusting out his jaw.

Penny let out a low, vibrating cry of anger.

'And mine!' she insisted. 'But let's move on to something else. How about your rotten little plot to cheat my father over the sale of Waterford Hall?'

In the silence that followed she distinctly heard the ticking of the grandfather clock in the hall and the wild, uneven thudding of her own heart. Josh's features looked grim and almost distorted, as he stared back at her, and she had a panic-stricken moment when she wondered if she had gone too far.

'What did you say?' demanded Josh in a dangerous voice.

She glanced nervously towards the door and swallowed hard. Her eyes darted rapidly away, avoiding Josh's gaze.

'I said it was my business about Richard,' she muttered.

'No, not that,' replied Josh grimly. 'If I'm going to be called a cheat, you can at least have the guts to look me in the eye as you say it, Penny.'

His fingers caught her by the chin and turned her face around to his. She blinked rapidly, overwhelmed by the realisation that what she had said probably spelled the end of her relationship with Josh. But there was no real hostility in his gaze. It was cool, unflustered, direct, as if he was trying to persuade her to stay calm. Yet some demon of wounded pride made her lash out.

'I hate you, Josh!' she flared. 'I think you're a cheat and a liar and an opportunist!'

Josh flinched as if she had struck him, but his cool gaze did not waver.

'Setting aside this matter of your father and your uncle,' he demanded reasonably, 'have I ever given you reason to suppose that I was a cheat and a liar?'

Penny gulped for breath and fought down a sob.

'How can I set it aside?' she protested furiously. 'It's so important, so——'

'Answer me, Penny,' he insisted, still fixing her with that piercing green gaze. 'Have I?'

She twisted free.

'No!' she cried grudgingly.

He let out a long, uneven breath and gripped her by the shoulders.

'And yet you believe I'm some lowdown, un-scrupulous son of a gun, just on the word of an old woman who's wandering in her mind?'

'She may be wandering when it comes to knowing what year it is,' retorted Penny, turning her head away from him. 'But she's sharp enough when it comes to talking about people.'

Josh brushed that aside.

'Maybe,' he agreed indifferently. 'But that's not the point. The point is that I've never betrayed you, Penny, so why can't you just agree to trust me? Your father's dead and gone and your uncle's alive and well, but with no particular interest in knowing you. Can't you just accept that and let the whole matter slide?'

'No!' she retorted, swinging back to face him. 'I want to know what's going on, Josh. I want to know what you were up to!'

Josh crumpled a piece of paper violently in his hands and flung it across the room.

'Believe me, Penny,' he said with a sigh, 'there are times when it's better not to know what people are up to, even when it's somebody you love.'

'I don't care,' retorted Penny defiantly, sticking out her chin. 'I still want to know.'

He rose to his feet and paced across the room. When he reached the window, he set his palms on the sill and gazed at the lush green garden outside.

'You know, when I took over this property,' he mused, 'it was a real mess. All the antique furniture had been sold off piece by piece and the plasterwork was crumbling. Even that garden out there was nothing but a jungle of weeds as high as your shoulder.'

'Well, that's very interesting,' said Penny coolly. 'But you're wasting your time trying to change the subject, Josh. I want to know what happened between you and the Eliots and why you lied to me and hid things from me.'

'Do you?' he asked, turning to face her. His expression hardened. 'Well, that's a shame, honey, because I'm not going to tell you.'

Penny took a slow, deep breath and felt a sense of misery so piercing that it was all she could do not to cry out.

'And that's all you've got to say on the subject?' she demanded.

He hesitated. A muscle twitched sharply in his cheek and for a moment she thought he was going to cross the room and sweep her into his arms. But instead he simply looked out of the window again.

'No,' he said with difficulty. 'I've got one more thing to say. Whatever I've done or whatever you think I've done, Penny, I love you. And the only thing I'm concerned about is your happiness.'

'It's not enough, Josh!' she choked. 'I'm tired of being treated like a child or a fool. You're as bad as my mother—she always thought she knew what was best for me too. She wouldn't talk to me about my father, she didn't even tell me that I was an American citizen. Maybe she thought she was protecting me, but all her protection ever did was hurt me. And now you're doing the same thing. I want to know the truth, Josh! I'm sick of all the lies and evasions.'

He remained rigid and silent, with his back to her. A lump rose in her throat and she bit her lip, fighting back tears. Then with a small, impatient cry she darted across the room and seized his arm. Pulling him round to face her, she stared straight at him.

'Why don't you say something?' she shouted. 'Why don't you defend yourself? Do you deny that you foreclosed on the mortgage?'

'No,' replied Josh grimly.

'Do you deny that you hid my uncle's existence from me?'

'No.'

Absurdly, Penny longed for him to say something, to shout, to rage, to defend himself, even to accuse her in some way. But he simply preserved an obstinate silence. Clutching his arm, she shook him as a terrier shakes a rat.

'If you don't explain to me, I'll leave you!' she threatened.

Josh clenched his teeth and stared at her in stony disbelief.

'So that's what our relationship is worth to you, is it?' he sneered. 'You won't just agree to drop the matter and trust me?'

'No!' cried Penny.

'Then leave!' he retorted savagely, thrusting her aside.

And without a backward glance, he strode out of the room.

CHAPTER NINE

PENNY stood outside the handsome wrought-iron gates
and looked up at the majestic brick house in front of
her. Biting her lip, she took a firmer hold on her small
overnight bag and turned back to face her companion.

'Well, thanks for the ride, Laney,' she said with a catch
in her voice. 'I guess I should say goodbye now.'

Against the backdrop of French-style mansions and
the gleaming blue water of Charleston Harbour, Laney
looked more modern and irreverent than ever. She was
wearing purple crushed cotton trousers with an orange
top and an outrageous purple straw hat. But most of
her usual bounce seemed to have subsided.

'Are you sure you know what you're doin', honey?'
she demanded for the tenth time. 'Why, I could just spit
when I think of you leavin' and goin' back to Sydney.
You know, I graduate next summer and I was lookin'
forward to havin' you around Clarksville. Besides, you
and Josh made a mighty fine couple. Are you sure this
ain't just some stupid quarrel you've gotten yourselves
into that really don't mean a damned thing?'

'Don't, Laney,' begged Penny, taking a long, uneven
breath. 'I'm sure.'

Laney shrugged unhappily.

'Kinda weird, thinkin' you had an uncle here all this
time and you never knew it,' she commented. 'But I can
understand why you want to see him before you leave.
Now, are you sure you don't want me to come up to the
house with you?'

'No, thanks,' said Penny regretfully. 'I think I'd better
tackle this on my own. But you've been wonderful—I'm
really going to miss you.'

'I'll miss you too, honey.'

The two girls embraced, and Laney's purple hat was knocked off into the road.

'Oh, shoot!' she cried, retrieving it and wiping it on her leg. 'Well, if you change your mind, Penny, you just call me up and I'll be real happy to drive back and get you.'

'OK,' agreed Penny. 'Bye, Laney.'

'Adios.'

Penny watched the other girl stride along the Battery until she reached her car and climbed inside. Then with a feeling of vague apprehension, she turned back to the gate. Any pleasure she might have felt at the thought of meeting her uncle had completely evaporated. In fact, she didn't even expect to like Richard Eliot. After all, he had helped to snatch Waterford Hall away from her own father and he was probably just as greedy and unscrupulous as Josh Miller himself. But Richard was still her uncle. And, having come halfway across the world in search of her roots, she was determined at least to set eyes on him. Her fingers hesitated on the rough brickwork, then strayed over highly polished brass. Screwing up her face, she rang the bell.

Its noisy clang reverberated through the entire yard. She had expected one of those discreet little remote-controlled buzzers that opened gates without human intervention. Instead there was a long pause, while she fanned herself with her airline ticket and shifted her weight from one foot to the other. Then a black man came striding round the corner of the house and stopped in the driveway. He advanced slowly and peered at her through the ornate metal grille. His face creased into a welcoming smile.

'Why, it's Miss Owen, ain't it? Didn't I see you here yesterday, ma'am? You're Mr Josh's fiancée, ain't you?'

Penny winced. So much had happened in the last twenty-four hours that it was hard to believe that it was only yesterday she had stood here with Josh beside her. Yet the thought of trying to explain any of it sent such a sharp, twisting sensation of misery through her that she simply nodded mutely.

'What can I do for you, ma'am?' asked the gardener pleasantly.

Penny let out her breath in a rush.

'Could I see Mr Richard Eliot, please?' she asked.

'Why, surely, ma'am. If you'll just step inside, I'll go find him for you. I believe he's out on the tennis court.'

She followed him up the driveway to the front porch of the house, where he offered her a seat in a rocking chair and scratched his head in a perplexed fashion.

'There ain't nobody inside the house right now, ma'am,' he apologised. 'And I don't have a key, but if you'd like to wait but a moment, I'll get Mr Richard for you.'

Left alone, Penny sank into the gleaming grey rocking chair and let out a long, unsteady sigh. Up to this moment her rage had sustained her, but now she was feeling an uncharacteristic urge to burst into tears. Her flight from Waterford Hall had caused no problems. Josh had not run after her—and anyway, she thought hastily, she didn't even want him to! The airline had offered her a seat on a flight leaving before midnight and Laney had been willing to drive her to Charleston. In fact, nothing in the world had stood in the way of her departure. Nothing except the aching sense of misery that seemed to be rising in her throat and threatening to choke her. She felt as shocked and horrified as if someone had pushed her out of a plane without a parachute or as if the ground had given way beneath her feet. Josh Miller, the man she had loved and trusted, had betrayed her. The mere thought of him now sent a stab of pain coursing through her, as sharp and unwanted as a persistent toothache. And why she should bother coming to meet his old pal Richard Eliot, who was probably just as greedy and heartless as Josh himself, she couldn't imagine! Except that just possibly Richard might have some wonderful explanation to offer that would prove Josh

wasn't as guilty as he seemed... Oh, Penny, you fool!
she told herself scathingly.

In a desperate attempt to avoid having to think, she
turned her attention to the porch where she was sitting.
With its grey-painted rocking chairs, its traditional swing
and its luxuriant potted palms and ferns, it provided a
cool and inviting refuge from the heat. And the house
itself looked equally welcoming. The brass doorknob and
the lion-headed knocker shone with polish and the glass
in the fanlight gleamed. On either side of the doorway
were two large Georgian-style windows, flanked by heavy
green wooden shutters. Through these windows Penny
caught a glimpse of a gracious interior filled with an-
tiques. Yet there was proof enough that this was no mere
museum, but a cheerful family home. Beside the front
door a skateboard lay propped carelessly against a tub
of scarlet salvias and a baseball mitt was half hidden
under an empty potato chip packet. Even if Richard Eliot
is an ogre, thought Penny grudgingly, he's certainly made
a beautiful home for his family.

'Good afternoon, ma'am. How may I help you?' enquired a low, pleasant voice.

Jolted out of her thoughts, Penny rose to her feet with
a cry of surprise. The man who was confronting her
didn't look like an ogre; he looked like a perfectly
friendly middle-aged attorney. Crisp grey curls covered
his head, his nose was long and straight and his blue
eyes were shrewd and vivid. In spite of the casual white
tennis clothes, he had an air of dignity and purpose about
him, as if he were accustomed to being immediately in
command of any situation. Stretching out one lean
brown hand, he smiled at her.

'I'm Richard Eliot,' he said. 'And you are——?'

'P-Penny,' she stammered, caught off guard. 'Penny
Owen.'

His handshake was firm and warm. Penny was dismayed to feel an instinctive liking for him.

'Penny Owen,' he repeated, frowning thoughtfully. 'And Leroy tells me you're engaged to Josh Miller. Is that right?'

'Yes. No. I mean... Oh, well, I was engaged to Josh Miller, but I've just broken it off. But that's not why I've come here. You see, I believe you're my uncle!'

'Your uncle?' echoed Richard incredulously. 'I'm afraid there must be some mistake, ma'am. There are no Owens in my family.'

'I took my mother's surname,' explained Penny hastily. 'My father was William C. Eliot from Waterford Hall.'

He stared at her, aghast.

'You're Bill's daughter?' he asked.

She nodded eagerly, hungry for some kind of display of family affection. But Richard did not kiss her or exclaim delightedly over her. He simply stood frowning thoughtfully down at her and then abruptly opened the front door wide.

'You'd better come in,' he said curtly.

She followed him into a hallway with a floor of dark, polished wood and an elegant, free-flying spiral staircase. The walls were covered to waist height in a white-panelled dado and above that there was a discreet gold and white striped wallpaper. Against this hung several portraits of men in wigs and knee-breeches and women in clinging, filmy dresses. A grandfather clock ticked steadily in a corner and a carved wooden settee with gold brocade covers was set with military precision in the centre of one wall. But once again the perfection of an Adam mansion was softened by the unmistakable signs of family life. A majestic blue and white Chinese vase standing on an antique drop-leaf table had a couple of Nintendo computer games leaning against it and there was a crumpled candy wrapper on the floor below. Richard Eliot picked up the wrapper with a sigh and opened a door leading into a wood-panelled study.

'Sit down, Miss Owen,' he invited. 'And tell me what brings you here.'

Penny smiled uncertainly and sank into a gold brocade wing-backed chair.

'Please call me Penny,' she replied, wondering how to begin.

Somehow Richard's manner was more wary than welcoming, and she had the uneasy feeling that he would much prefer her to vanish from the house than to stay and chat. Twisting her hands together, she looked him frankly in the eye.

'I won't keep you long,' she said. 'I'll be flying back to Australia tonight and I've only come to say hello to you.'

'You don't want anything from me, then?' he asked with a touch of surprise.

'No, of course not!' she retorted indignantly. 'Why should I? I didn't even know you existed until this morning.'

Richard flung the crumpled candy wrapper into the waste paper basket and looked at her keenly. Some of the tension seemed to vanish from his manner, as if he was reassured by what he saw.

'Tell me about yourself,' he urged in a more encouraging tone. 'Where you grew up, how you came to be here and so on.'

He listened in silence while Penny told him about her childhood in Sydney, her mother's struggle to make a pleasant home in the tiny apartment they shared, her astonishment and joy at receiving her father's legacy, the shock of losing her new home in the hurricane. When at last she faltered to a stop, he gazed at her shrewdly.

'You didn't say anything about your engagement to Josh Miller,' he pointed out.

Penny's mouth quivered dangerously.

'That was an error of judgement,' she said with dignity. 'So I ended it.'

'Why?'

The curt monosyllable cut through the air like a knife. To her annoyance, she saw that Richard was eyeing her critically as if her only error of judgement lay in breaking the engagement. Stung into response, she told the truth.

'Because he cheated my father out of Waterford Hall!' she retorted.

'What?' he demanded incredulously, advancing towards her. 'Who told you such a thing?'

Penny flinched, but raised her head.

'Louella McGregor,' she muttered.

He slammed his fist into the palm of his other hand.

'That woman is ninety years old and half crazy!' he exclaimed. 'Do you mean to tell me you've broken off your engagement to a fine man like Josh Miller because of some hyped-up rubbish you heard from her?'

'It's not rubbish!' began Penny. 'Josh admitted——' But Richard cut in.

'Is there no end to the trouble that man has caused?' he demanded.

'Josh?' echoed Penny in bewilderment.

'No! William C. Eliot,' he snapped. 'Why didn't Josh tell you the truth about him?'

She looked baffled.

'What do you mean?' she demanded. 'What is there to tell?'

He looked at her grimly.

'How much do you know about your father?' he demanded.

'N-not much,' admitted Penny. 'Just that he was handsome and charming and everybody liked him.'

'And everybody covered up for him,' continued Richard sourly. 'Well, in my view, it's time you learned the truth about your wonderful father, honey. People have been covering up for far too long. And there's one man who's got the right and the duty to tell you.'

He strode purposefully across to the telephone.

'W-what are you doing?' faltered Penny.

'Calling Josh Miller. And you're going to sit there until he arrives, young lady, or I'll tie you to the chair!'

It was an hour and a half before Josh came, and during that time Penny had plenty of opportunity to think. Her uncle took her out to the tennis court to meet her aunt Nancy and the two boys, Alan and Chris. Everybody was friendly and full of questions about Australia, but Penny was anxious not to spoil their Saturday activity. She urged them several times to continue their game of tennis, and eventually they gave in. With a vast beach umbrella shielding her from the sun and a cold drink at her elbow, she sat on the sidelines to watch. But she could give little attention to the thwack of balls on racquets or the cries of 'Fifteen love!' that filled the air. For her brain was racing with other thoughts.

The volcanic rage that had sent her storming out of Waterford Hall and across to Laney's house to beg a ride to Charleston had now subsided, and in its place came a nagging sense of doubt. Penny was no fool, and she could see clearly enough that Richard Eliot had not worshipped his brother William, as most people did. Exactly what his veiled hints about her father really meant, she could not fathom. But the fact that he had made them at all left her feeling thoroughly uneasy. Were there two sides to the story of the sale of Waterford Hall? And was it really likely that Josh Miller would have exploited her father?

She tried to review everything she knew about Josh, to draw up a logical balance sheet of his good and bad qualities. But it was impossible to think of him in those terms. All she could summon up was a series of vivid pictures. Josh by the river bank sliding her over his shoulder and laughing, Josh carrying her up to bed in the lamplight, Josh, wild-eyed and drenched to the skin, crushing her against him in the middle of the hurricane, Josh with a chainsaw and a four-wheel-drive challenging the devastation that surrounded him. I love him, she thought with a sudden, piercing clarity. He may be high-handed and secretive and the most infuriating man alive, but I love him. I don't believe he's capable of a single mean action. And, whatever he's concealing, it can't possibly be anything that discredits him. What's more, I'm going to tell him that when he comes.

This resolution made her feel a little better, but when the brass bell at the gate finally rang out through the garden again, she still experienced a sharp pang of apprehension. Josh was a proud man and she had insulted him. Even if she apologised, would anything ever heal the rift between them? Nervously she rose to her feet and cast a questioning glance at her uncle. He gave her a brief, reassuring nod.

'Go into the study and wait,' he ordered. 'I'll send Josh in to you. It's time you two thrashed things out and cleared the air.'

Five minutes later the door of the study opened and Josh stepped silently in. Penny's hands twisted into knots and she stared at him in dismay. He was wearing the grim, furious expression that she had seen so often in the early weeks of their relationship when their feud about Merivale had been at its height. Even when he closed the door, there was a suppressed violence in the action, as if he were barely holding his anger in check.

'Well?' he said coldly. 'Richard seems to think it's time I told you truth, but are you sure you want to know it?'

Penny gazed back at him steadily. She had expected to feel upset or annoyed or even excited by this meeting. Instead she felt only a calm and lucid determination to set the record straight. Crossing the room, she took hold of his arms and gazed earnestly up into his face.

'Yes,' she said quietly. 'But before you do tell me, Josh, there's something I want to say. I've been thinking over everything that's happened, and I just want you to know that, whatever the truth is, I'm sorry that I didn't trust you. I had no business believing anything bad about

you, when my own experience should have shown me
that you couldn't do a mean thing if you tried.'

For an instant Josh's face remained set in its rigid lines
of hostility, then slowly the thaw set in. His scowling
black brows relaxed, his narrowed eyes widened and a
slow, exultant grin spread over his face.

'You know, one thing I'll say for you, Miss Penny,'
he drawled throatily. 'You may be a sassy, opinionated
little parcel of trouble that goes off like a packet of fire-
crackers whenever you lose your temper, but you're a
mighty good judge of character!'

His strong brown arms came around her and he
crushed her imperiously against him. Then turning her
mouth up to his, he kissed her long and hard. Penny let
her full weight relax against him, feeling a deep, primitive
joy flood through her as she tasted the freshness of his
mouth on hers and felt his strong, virile body pressed
against her. She could smell the spicy tang of his after-
shave and feel the swift, steady beating of his heart as
he held her tightly to him. For a long, long time she
stood there, arched into his embrace with her lips parted
sensually against his. But at last, with a low, trembling
sigh, she pulled free.

'Now tell me about my father,' she said firmly.

Josh groaned.

'Damn your father!' he retorted. 'He's not worth
knowing about anyways.'

'I'd already guessed that,' murmured Penny wryly.
'But I think I should know the truth.'

'You're sure?' he asked reluctantly.

'Yes.'

He paced across the room and then turned to face her.

'All right, Penny,' he said bluntly, 'I'll give it to you
straight. William C. Eliot was handsome and charming
and likeable, just the way you've been told. He was also
a con-man, a gambler and a drunk. He squandered his
own inheritance, embezzled the money your grandmother had set aside to put Richard through college and

served prison sentences for fraud in three different states. Is that enough for you, or should I go on?'

Penny stared at him, appalled. She opened her mouth to say, 'I don't believe you', but the words wouldn't come. For somehow, hideously, she did believe him.

'It all fits,' she murmured in a stunned voice. 'No wonder you acted so strangely when I told you I was William Eliot's daughter! A con-man and a drunk and...prison sentences?'

There was an edge of hysteria to her voice now, and Josh took her firmly by the shoulders and steered her across to the sofa.

'Oh, honey!' he said, pushing her into the seat and kneeling in front of her. 'I didn't want you to go through all this. That's why I didn't tell you before.'

'You mean you lied to protect me?' she demanded.

Her voice wobbled dangerously and she pressed her lips firmly together to avoid bursting into tears.

'Yes,' he agreed heavily. 'Hell, honey, I'm sorry, but I just couldn't bear to disappoint you like that. Every time you talked about your daddy, your face would light up like you were talking about Christmas. Bill Eliot didn't give you much, but at least he left you with an illusion. I didn't want to be the one to take it away.'

Penny was silent for a moment, fighting back tears.

'He left me Merivale,' she protested. 'And some money. He must have cared about me a bit.'

Josh rose to his feet and looked down at her.

'Penny, he didn't even leave you that,' he replied brutally. 'If you want the truth, you might as well have it all. Merivale belonged to your grandmother and she left everything in her will to your father. If he had lived, you can be damned sure he would have squandered that too. As it was, they both died in the fire, and even that was probably his fault. The firemen believe he fell asleep drunk with a cigarette in his hand and sent the whole place up in flames. What's worse, he didn't bother to leave a will at all, so you inherited the property simply

because you were his only child. Not because he gave a
damn about you.'

Penny looked crushed.

'How did anybody even know I existed, then, if he
didn't leave a will?' she demanded.

Josh shrugged uncomfortably.

'Well, I believe he once told Richard he'd left a
pregnant wife behind him in Australia,' he admitted.
'Richard insisted that William's lawyer try to trace you,
although he didn't want to have any contact with you
himself. Perhaps he thought you'd be just like your
father. Anyway, I imagine he'll feel differently now that
he's met you.'

For a moment Penny was silent, pressing her lips
firmly together to stop them trembling.

'I see,' she said at last. 'And what about the sale of
Waterford Hall? I suppose my father comes out of that
pretty badly too, does he?'

Josh winced.

'Honey, there's no need——' he began.

'Yes, there is!' cut in Penny fiercely. 'Hearing all this
is terrible, Josh, it just tears me apart, but I've got to
know the truth. What really happened?'

He looked at her tense, determined face and gave a
sigh of resignation.

'Your father had borrowed and borrowed from me,'
he explained. 'And he never made any repayments. In
the end your grandmother came to me, begged me to
buy Waterford Hall and took me into her confidence.
It seemed your father had been embezzling money from
a firm in Virginia and if he didn't pay it back real smart
he'd go to prison again. The only way he could raise the
money was to sell the estate, but he wouldn't agree to
it. She pleaded with me to call in the mortgages so he
would have to sell, and Richard agreed that it was the
only thing to do. I gave William a fair price for the place,
but that wasn't the story that he told.'

Penny gave a low, bitter laugh.

'All those years that I wondered about my father,' she said ruefully. 'It never once occurred to me that he was a common criminal. I'm beginning to see why my mother never wanted his name mentioned in front of her.'

Josh nodded.

'Well, that's hardly surprising,' he agreed. 'Seeing as how he cleaned out her bank account before he left her.'

She did a double-take.

'How do you know?' she demanded.

A ghost of a smile hovered on his lips.

'I telephoned her after you left this morning,' he said. 'And we got to talking about everything under the sun. She seems like a real nice woman.'

'But why did you phone her?' asked Penny, looking baffled.

Josh looked·uncomfortable.

'I wanted to make sure that if I didn't manage to catch you at the airport, at least she could give you a message from me when you got home,' he replied offhandedly.

'Oh,' said Penny. And then, in a carefully casual voice, 'Were you going to try and catch me at the airport?'

'Well, the thought did cross my mind,' admitted Josh carelessly.

Her lips curved into the hesitant beginnings of a smile.

'So what was the message?' she asked.

He stared with apparent fascination at a shelf of leather-bound law reports. He cleared his throat and then spoke in the tone he might have used to discuss boll weevil in his cotton plants.

'Oh. Just that I loved you more than any woman I'd ever known and I still wanted to marry you on any terms you liked,' he said stiffly.

Penny's lips quivered.

'Oh, Josh!' she breathed, darting to her feet and rushing into his arms.

There was a moment's silence as he held her close and then there was the sound of a muffled sob.

'Honey, what is it?' demanded Josh in an appalled voice. 'Don't you want to marry me?'

'Yes, of course I do!' she gulped. 'But how can I after what you've just told me. Everybody in the County will be gossiping about how you've married a criminal's daughter and dragging your name in the mud.'

He took her arms and gave her a little shake.

'It wouldn't matter even if they were,' he said firmly. 'But they won't be, Penny. However foolish your grandmother was, she was always very careful about protecting the Eliots' good name, and so was Richard. And even your father, in his own strange way, seems to have cared about it. None of his prison sentences were served under his real name, so nobody in Williamsburg County has the faintest suspicion that he was anything worse than an unlucky investor. Except Brenda Sue.'

'Brenda Sue?' echoed Penny, aghast.

'Now don't fret,' urged Josh reassuringly. 'She doesn't know the full truth. I questioned her pretty carefully when we were down at Myrtle Beach, and what she does know can't do you much harm.'

She gave him a long, searching look.

'Josh, what were you and Brenda Sue doing down at Myrtle Beach together?' she demanded suspiciously.

He gave a low rumble of laughter.

'Well, not rolling in the hay together, honey, that's for sure,' he said. 'Although Brenda Sue did suggest it. As a matter of fact, she followed me down there and told me she had a proposal to make.'

'A proposal? What kind of a proposal?' asked Penny in alarm.

He smiled reminiscently.

'Well, she wanted me to drop you and go back to her. Or else she'd make public the contents of a file that the insurance company had compiled on your father.'

'What kind of file?' she demanded apprehensively.

'I don't blame you for looking worried,' said Josh. 'I was pretty damn worried myself when she told me that.

But it turned out not to be as bad as I feared. It seems the insurance company smelled a rat with a couple of claims that William Eliot had made. They were almost certainly bogus and an investigation had been launched, but your father died while it was still under way. In any case, they hadn't found enough evidence for a successful prosecution, so the file was marked CLOSED.'

Penny breathed again.

'Oh, Josh, that's such a relief to me,' she confessed. 'Not just about my father, but even more about you. I really thought you'd gone back to Brenda Sue at Myrtle Beach.'

He twined his fingers in her thick fair hair and, using it as a rope, drew her towards him.

'You insult me, Penny,' he murmured throatily. 'There's only been one woman for me for quite a while now. As a matter of fact, I think I fell in love with you the first minute I saw you.'

'Really?' she asked doubtfully.

'Sure,' agreed Josh, his eyes dancing with mischief. 'When I first saw you lying there on that bank by the river, with your hands over your eyes, begging me not to shoot you, that was it. I knew I'd never meet another woman in the world who'd make me laugh as much as that.'

'Thanks a lot!' cried Penny indignantly, struggling to escape from his grip.

But Josh's strong brown arms were locked around her as tightly as steel cables and his lips were stirring the most miraculous sensations as they touched her hair and her eyelids and the hollows of her throat.

'And I also knew I'd never meet a woman as sweet and loyal and giving as you,' he continued in a voice that was no longer teasing but resonant and full of passion. 'A woman who could face disaster like a pioneer and still come up smiling. A woman I'd be proud to have as my life's partner through thick and thin.'

'Oh, Josh,' murmured Penny shakily.

Putting up her fingers, she traced the strong outline of his jaw and mouth, then smiled at the tremor that went through his body.

'When did you really fall in love with me?' she persisted. 'Seriously.'

He caught her hand and kissed it.

'Hell, Penny,' he replied. 'I can't pinpoint the moment, but I'll tell you this. You really shook me up from the very first time I set eyes on you. When I carried you upstairs that first night—do you remember?—you were practically unconscious from the pethidine and I tripped when I put you on the bed. You gasped and sat up, and I knew right away that I'd hurt you. I didn't mean to kiss you, or maybe I just meant to kiss you in a friendly way to reassure you. But what I wasn't prepared for was the way the whole earth seemed to tilt on its axis once I touched you. You looked so vulnerable, so feminine, so desirable, lying there in the lamplight. I just wanted to sweep you into my arms and engulf you, possess you, fight off every other man that ever thought of looking at you. I wanted to make you mine, Penny!'

She smiled wryly.

'You almost did, if I remember correctly,' she reminded him.

'I know,' admitted Josh. 'And I can't tell you how horrified I was with myself. After all, you were barely conscious and you wouldn't really have known what you were doing. I told myself it was just a trick of my emotions that didn't mean a damned thing, but I was even more horrified the next morning when I found that I wanted you just as badly. I'd had women before, but I sensed right away that this was something different. Because it wasn't just your body that I wanted, Penny. I wanted to know all about you. Every thought that went on in your head, what sort of things you liked to do, where you'd grown up, who your parents were——'

'And then I told you William Eliot was my father,' pointed out Penny drily.

Josh caught his breath.

'Yeah,' he agreed. 'Now that was a tricky one. In a way I was glad. I told myself you were probably just like your old man—nothing but an opportunist out for a good time at other people's expense. And yet half of me knew all the time that you weren't a bit like that. Deep down, I always knew you were honest and loyal and sincere. But it made me feel safer to kid myself that you were extravagant and impulsive and unreliable.'

'Why?' demanded Penny, looking baffled.

Josh sighed.

'Because it gave me an excuse to back off from this scary sort of intimacy that seemed to be developing between us,' he explained. 'I'd never met a woman before who made me feel I wanted to make a total commitment to her. And I hadn't had the kind of background that made me feel comfortable with tenderness. My parents were pretty tough on me, and the Air Force doesn't exactly bring out a guy's emotional side. Besides, I wasn't a bit sure that you felt anything like the same attraction and involvement that I did. After all, you slammed the door in my face every time I came to visit. That used to make me as mad as fire.'

Penny chuckled.

'Well, you made me as mad as fire, trying to buy my house every time you saw me,' she retorted. 'Why didn't you just invite me to a movie or something? Be nice to me?'

He looked perplexed.

'I don't know,' he admitted. 'I guess I wanted to feel I was in control of things. I should have realised I could just as easily control Hurricane Janice as you. Anyway, I finally figured that getting the door slammed in my face once a week wasn't the way to go.'

She gave another gurgle of laughter.

'So you persuaded Wilma to invite me to the Cotillion Ball?' she prompted.

'That's right,' said Josh in an aggrieved voice. 'And I was just telling you that I was in love with you when Brenda Sue showed up.'

'Josh!' she protested. 'That's not true! You never said anything about being in love with me then.'

'Well, that was what I meant!' exclaimed Josh in an exasperated voice. 'Hell, I thought you knew that, Penny! You didn't expect me to come right out and say it, did you?'

'Oh, Josh!' wailed Penny. 'It would have saved a lot of trouble if you had. I thought you were just using me to get even with Brenda Sue.'

'Penny,' he murmured softly, 'the minute I got to know you, I found Brenda Sue about as bright, appealing and lovable as a Barbie doll. If you want to know the truth, it was a big relief to me when she took up with Greg Alden!'

Penny sighed.

'Well, I wish I'd known,' she insisted. 'I wouldn't have gone off to Myrtle Beach if you'd told me that.'

He shrugged.

'Maybe it's a good thing you did,' he said. 'Because that's when I realised that I didn't just want to get to know you, I wanted to marry you too. But of course, the minute I found you, you shot off again!'

She looked guilty.

'Well, I wouldn't have done if you hadn't been so damned secretive about everything,' she retorted.

'I was only trying to protect you, honey,' he protested, turning her face up to his and gazing down at her.

'I know, Josh,' said Penny, returning his gaze. 'But it was pure torment, thinking you were involved with Brenda Sue. I know you were being the the strong, silent male and trying to shelter me, but I'd rather know the truth than suffer all that worry and uncertainty. So no more secrets in future. Please?'

'No more secrets,' agreed Josh.

His lips met hers, warm, demanding, insistent. The room seemed to spin away from them, and Penny floated blissfully in space, conscious only of the joy of having Josh's arms around her and Josh's body pressed hard against her. Time had no further meaning until at last there was a knock at the door.

'Come in,' called Josh reluctantly.

Richard Eliot stepped inside with a look of sly amusement on his face.

'Well, Penny,' he said challengingly, 'Nancy tells me she can't keep lunch waiting a minute longer, so you've got two choices. Should I open the Bollinger champagne to celebrate your engagement, or drive you to the airport?'

Penny let out a low ripple of laughter and snuggled deep into Josh's broad chest.

'I think you'd better open the champagne, Uncle Richard,' she replied.

It was late afternoon when they arrived back at Waterford Hall. The sun was already sinking low in the brassy sky like a red ball of fire and the chimney sweeps were flying in twittering arcs between the live oak trees. At the end of the avenue Waterford Hall stood proud and dignified amid its ravaged gardens.

'Isn't it nice to be home?' said Penny with a sigh, as the car drew up on the gravel drive in front of the house.

'It sure is,' agreed Josh, shooting her a meaningful glance. 'But it's been a long day. Don't you think we should go to bed early?'

She grinned.

'Why not?' she replied archly. 'I'm pretty tired. I could do with some sleep.'

'Sleep,' murmured Josh with another searing glance, 'is the last thing you're going to get, sweetheart.'

Five minutes later she found herself sprawled in the huge fourposter bed upstairs. The fiery glow of the sun slanted in through the tall windows and turned Josh's

naked body to bronze. His dark hair gleamed in a bur-
nished mane above his lean, craggy face and his eyes
were no more than glittering points of light as he gazed
down at her. There was an urgent, passionate savagery
in that look which made her body arch sensually towards him under the thin covers. His hand paused,
grasping the edge of the crocheted white bedspread.

'Oh, Penny,' he murmured throatily, 'I've been waiting
so long for this moment.'

She smiled uncertainly, feeling oddly shy.

'You make it sound as if it's the very first time for
us,' she whispered.

'It is,' he said in a voice harsh with pent-up need.
'The very first time without barriers of suspicion and
mistrust. And you're going to give yourself to me completely and utterly, Penny. Now!'

His hand twisted fiercely and he flung back the covers,
exposing her slim, naked body to his gaze. As sensually
as some prowling jungle creature, he stretched out on
the bed beside her and cupped one white breast in his
warm palm. She closed her eyes and swallowed as his
fingers moved slowly and erotically over the tip of her
nipple, brushing it into an agonised arousal. Then he
bent his head and his mouth followed where his fingers
had led the way. She gasped as he drew the taut, hard
bud of flesh into his mouth and sucked tantalisingly on
it. She tried to struggle up into his arms and return his
caresses, but with a growl of amusement he pushed her
back.

'Lie still,' he ordered, 'and let me take you.'

She had not believed that lovemaking could be so de-
liciously, tormentingly fulfilling. Soon every curve and
hollow and surface of her body was tingling and writhing
under Josh's expert touch. And the satisfying power and
weight of his body as he moved against her woke incredible sensations inside her. Whimpering softly in her
throat, she pressed herself against him, glorying in his
hard, muscular body, the primitive male odour of him,

the fierce, insistent throb of his heartbeat beneath his
tanned skin. All she wanted, all she had ever wanted,
was to be his. If only he would take her, penetrate her,
fill her with his warm, hard, masculine strength, she felt
she would dissolve into a blinding starburst of fulfilment.
Catching him fiercely by his hair, she drew his head down
to hers and kissed him with long, hard, sensual force.

'Take me, Josh,' she breathed. 'I love you so much.
Oh, please, please, take me!'

She heard his deep, harsh intake of breath, then his
lips paused against her ear, sending tremors of warmth
pulsating through her body.

'I love you too, Penny,' he muttered. 'You're going
to be mine, now and forever.'

Then, with a low growl of satisfaction, he drove into
her. It was a fierce, stormy lovemaking that sent them
rolling wildly across the bed, overturning a lamp and
tearing a sheet to shreds. But they clung together with
all the passion of two fiery natures, determined to slake
their deep, primitive need for each other. And in the
midst of that furious crescendo of love, Penny felt
fulfilment surge up inside her, retreat and then come
thudding back so that she cried aloud.

'Josh! Josh! Oh, my love, I need you so much!'

And when he caught her and crushed her against him
and whispered her name it was all the reply she needed.

An hour or so later, when they had both returned to
earth enough to talk about such mundane things as fixing
dinner and buying another lamp, Penny surprised Josh
by suddenly jumping out of bed and scrambling into her
clothes.

'Where are you going?' he demanded.

'There's something I want to do before it gets dark,'
she explained. 'In fact, you can come and help. Just come
out to the front lawn whenever you're ready.'

She picked up his T-shirt and jeans and flung them at
him. Josh shrugged resignedly and got dressed.

'Whatever you say, ma'am,' he said with a sigh.

When he came out of the front door five minutes later, he found Penny crouching in the middle of the heart-shaped flower-bed in the centre of the lawn.

'What in blazes are you doing?' he demanded.

She looked up and smiled, her face transfigured by the last rays of the setting sun.

'Just planting out those seedlings we bought in Charleston,' she explained, rising to her feet and brushing off the soil from her fingers. 'I want to make sure that there's always love in this house.'

She stood poised for a moment, like a diver about to take a plunge, then took a flying leap towards him. But, as she reached the edge of the flower-bed, she lost her balance and lurched towards him. His arms closed around her and he held her tightly against him as he kissed her. Then he smiled his slow, mischievous smile at her.

'Oh, I think we can take care of that,' he promised confidently.

The truth often hurts . . .

Sometimes it heals

Critically injured in a car accident, Liz Danvers insists her family read
the secret diaries she has kept for years – revealing a lifetime of courage,
sacrifice and a great love. Liz knew the truth would be painful for her
daughter Sage to face, as the diaries would finally explain the agonising
choices that have so embittered her most cherished child.

Available now priced £4.99

W⊕RLDWIDE

Available from Boots, Martins, John Menzies,
W.H. Smith and other paperback stockists.

Also available from Mills and Boon Reader Service,
P.O. Box 236, Thornton Road, Croydon, Surrey CR9 3RU

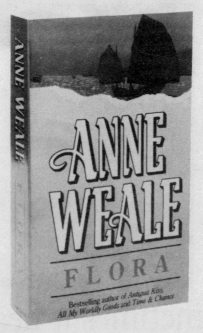

4 FREE

Romances and 2 FREE gifts just for you!

You can enjoy all the heartwarming emotion of true love for FREE! Discover the heartbreak and the happiness, the emotion and the tenderness of the modern relationships in Mills & Boon Romances.

We'll send you 4 captivating Romances as a special offer from Mills & Boon Reader Service, along with the chance to have 6 Romances delivered to your door each month.

Claim your FREE books and gifts overleaf...

An irresistible offer from Mills & Boon

Here's a personal invitation from Mills & Boon Reader Service, to become a regular reader of Romances. To welcome you, we'd like you to have 4 books, a CUDDLY TEDDY and a special MYSTERY GIFT absolutely FREE.

Then you could look forward each month to receiving 6 brand new Romances, delivered to your door, postage and packing free! Plus our free newsletter featuring author news, competitions, special offers and much more.

This invitation comes with no strings attached. You may cancel or suspend your subscription at any time, and still keep your free books and gifts.

It's so easy. Send no money now. Simply fill in the coupon below and post it to -
Reader Service, FREEPOST, PO Box 236, Croydon, Surrey CR9 9EL.

- - - - - - - - - - - - - - `NO STAMP REQUIRED` - - - - - - - - - - - - - -

Free Books Coupon

Yes! Please rush me my 4 free Romances and 2 free gifts! Please also reserve me a Reader Service subscription. If I decide to subscribe I can look forward to receiving 6 brand new Romances each month for just £9.60, postage and packing free. If I choose not to subscribe I shall write to you within 10 days - I can keep the books and gifts whatever I decide. I may cancel or suspend my subscription at any time. I am over 18 years of age.

Name Mrs/Miss/Ms/Mr _____ EP18R

Address _____

_____

Postcode_____ Signature _____

Offer expires 31st May 1992. The right is reserved to refuse an application and change the terms of this offer. Readers overseas and in Eire please send for details. Southern Africa write to Book Services International Ltd, P.O. Box 41654, Craighall, Transvaal 2024. You may be mailed with offers from other reputable companies as a result of this application.
If you would prefer not to share in this opportunity, please tick box. ☐

mps
MAILING
PREFERENCE
SERVICE